irlanda

Espido Freire

irlanda

translated by Toshiya Kamei

FAIRY TALE REVIEW · PRESS
2011

FAIRY TALE REVIEW · PRESS
2011

EDITOR: Kate Bernheimer

ART DIRECTION: Jordan Cox and Tara Reeser,
English Department's Publications Unit at Illinois State University

COVER ART: Nicoletta Ceccoli

RIGHTS HELD: World English in all forms

WWW.FAIRYTALEREVIEW.COM

Distribution by Small Press Distribution
WWW.SPDBOOKS.ORG

Fairy Tale Review Press gratefully acknowledges the Program for Cultural
Cooperation at the University of Minnesota and Spain's Special Ministry of
Culture for their generous support of this publication.

ISBN: 0-9799954-4-2; 978-0-9799954-4-6

How would I begin to recall you, dead as you are, you willingly, passionately dead? Was it as soothing as you imagined, or was not being alive still far from being dead?

Rainer Maria Rilke

1

Sagrario died in May, after much suffering. She was buried after a service at the packed church. Many flowers lay on her grave during the first week, but they soon disappeared. Every day Nena and I went to the cemetery to clear away the mourning wreaths that had wilted. Nena shooed away the cats that sneaked in under the entrance gate, gathered palm leaves and flowers, and asked me if any of them were poisonous. We carefully arranged them together to dry in my flower press. My mother wanted to make a scrapbook with these flowers, the ribbons, and the strand she had cut from my sister's hair.

Things went back to the way they had been before, although we saw my parents wandering aimlessly around the house, as if they had too many things to do. I went back to the room I had shared with Sagrario and slept with my face turned away from the empty bed. We treated Nena as if she would be the next one to die and stopped letting her play in the street, because we were afraid of kidnappers and cars.

Whenever Nena and I got home from school, we found my mother in front of the empty bed in my room, seated on the bench she had barely left in the last few months. She would be praying, or reading a letter from her sister. She looked up at Nena and me.

"I need to send you away," she said, and I was scared. I was certain that she too saw Sagrario when she sat there, and that wasn't fair of Sagrario.

Then my mother wiped her tears. I breathed easier because she had no idea that my sister visited me at night and danced in circles. She had her own suffering in mind and wanted to spare us her pain.

The shop windows of the large department stores were filled with bright-colored clothes, beachwear, and outdoor gear. The funeral flowers dried in my press, and my mother made a scrapbook with Sagrario's photos in the diary where my sister had written down what she saw and thought. Nena removed the flowers from the press and looked at them against the light.

"They were from the caretaker's bouquet. And the nuns at school sent these red peonies. They're not poisonous, are they?"

"No," I said. "They aren't poisonous."

My aunt's letters kept arriving, and my mother watched us and shook her head. Other times, when Nena had already gone to bed, she called to me and read aloud a passage from Sagrario's diary. I knew my sister didn't want us going through her things, but with the flowers, her ribbons, and her photos, her diary had become as much my mother's book as hers, and my mother found a melancholy pleasure in deciphering Sagrario's difficult handwriting. When Nena was in bed, I sat next to my mother and listened to her while she caressed my hair.

"Listen to this, Natalia."

This constant fading in and out destroys me and keeps me from look-
ing cheerful in front of my family. I often think about what these
places will be like when I'm gone. If I could just get out of bed and
walk again, I'd stop feeling like I'm turning into a different person
every minute. But nothing is clear, except this constant change inside
me and the stillness of everything around me.

My mother stopped reading, tears welling up.

"My poor daughter."

Soon we learned my sister's secret words by heart. She used ini-
tials for our names, which disappeared gradually when she started
focusing more on herself as she steadily drew closer to death. I
always opened the scrapbook to the same place, a half-written
page that beckoned me like faraway church bells.

I read the poems in the book they gave me and love is in all of them,
surrounded by mist, dream, dust, stars. Everything is so beautiful, but
I don't think love is anything like that. Love could appear on a clear
day when I sit on a bench with a book, and I watch pigeons peck at
breadcrumbs in the grass. Then he sits next to me with his book, and
my heart starts pounding. It stops beating, or beats so fast I can't keep
reading. I look at him. He returns my glance and brings my hand to
his lips. He kisses it. This is love.

Now that her heart had stopped beating forever, I wished
Sagrario had found the love she wrote about. She wouldn't be
alone in the dance of death, only her turtle trailing after her, and
wouldn't attract the wicked souls jumping and circling and giving
in to the dance's dark pleasure. My mother took the diary away
from me and read it aloud. I listened, obedient.

Classes ended in early June, and I waited for my baby sister at
the school gate. Nena held a bundle of drawings with sober colors
and large handwriting. I had a pink report card with good grades
and an envelope with a letter to my parents in it. We smiled at

the bus driver, who, surprised, didn't smile back right away. I let Nena cross the street against a red light, running to get past cars that braked hard, tires screeching.

We were almost happy that we could spend the whole day at home. We would take long walks through the fields to pick plants for my herbarium, and maybe we would cheer up the house a bit for a while. The nights would get shorter, so would my nightmares, and I would be less haunted by the turtle that had tormented me since I was a little girl and by the last image of Sagrario's pale face among the pillows.

"Can we go to the public garden?" asked Nena.

"You're not allowed to pick plants there."

"Then why do they plant flowers?"

"Grown-ups do lots of useless things."

My mother was sitting in my room, two stacks of folded clothes on the bed.

From the door I asked, "Are you going to give Sagrario's clothes away?"

She shook her head. She combed Nena's hair with her fingers. "Not a day goes by that I don't receive a letter from my sister. She wants me to let you spend the summer there. Nena could stay with them and you'll be with your cousins in the country house. Go eat now. Wash your hands." She grabbed Nena by the wrist. "Don't you see how dirty they are?"

"Nobody lives in the country house anymore," I said, seating myself at the table.

"Your cousins and their friends are there. Your uncle wants to sell the property, and they want to fix it up a bit. You'll love it. I can't keep you in here any longer." She shook her head. "It's not a healthy environment for you. For either of you."

My father agreed. He slowly cut meat into pieces for Nena. She wasn't allowed to use a knife.

"Your aunt and uncle want you to stay with them. After they

sell the house, you won't have a chance to enjoy your summer like that."

After the meal, when we were doing the dishes, my father opened the letter that accompanied my report card. He read it with a frown, then left it on the table.

"Have you read what the nuns say?"

"No," I answered.

"They say you get distracted, you don't work well in a group, and you're unsociable. And they say perhaps you should show more interest in math. What do you think of that?"

"I should try harder in math," I admitted, looking down.

"They're so heartless. Of course you get distracted. I didn't even expect you to finish the term." He took my hands and hugged me. "Come here. You're a good student, a good daughter."

His voice was filled with tears. He held me close to him for a moment. Then I slipped into the living room, and Nena came closer to me.

"Who are they, aunt and uncle?" she asked.

"Mama's sister. Don't you remember? They were here for Sagrario's saint's day. She was a beautiful woman. She held you in her arms. She gave you the blue clown."

"They didn't come to the funeral?"

"No."

"Oh," she said, losing interest.

She didn't say anything else and spent the afternoon playing quietly. The phone rang and she rushed to answer it, as always, and my mother got there first, as always. Nena wasn't allowed to play with the phone.

"It was your aunt," my mother said. "She expects both of you tomorrow."

Nena thought nothing of it, but as the hours went by, she started pouting. That night she didn't stop crying, and she hugged my mother's knees, asking her not to send her away. My mother cried too.

"She's too young to spend the whole summer away from her parents," she decided. "But you're going, aren't you, honey? Don't make me look bad in front of my sister. They don't have animals in the house anymore, your aunt promised me. I'm going to pack your things. Don't you understand if you stay here all summer, it'll be as if nothing had changed, and I can't force myself to be strong? You know we need to do this."

I agreed in the end, because I kept tossing and turning all night and the turtle was coming back to haunt me. Also I wanted to please my mother. She smiled with relief and made me pack my things for the same day. I gathered my clothes and started ironing. It was the only chore I enjoyed. Ironing and taking care of my sisters. Nena had stretched out on the floor next to me, drawing.

"Now I remember aunt and uncle. They sent a white wreath with lilies and arum lilies like trumpets. Are lilies poisonous?"

"No," I said, almost out of habit. "But you shouldn't eat arum lilies."

She rested on her elbow and handed me her drawing.

"Look."

"What's this?" I raised my voice and tried to deceive my mother, who was walking down the hallway. "I see. Another princess sleeping in her coffin? Now she has to wait for the prince to come and kiss her."

"No," she said. "It's Sagrario. It's for you."

I put her drawing aside and stared at Nena. I pressed the tip of her nose with my finger, to make her smile, and I went back to my ironing. She lay down again.

"Natalia…"

"I'm busy right now."

"Tell me the story of when I was born."

"I've told you a thousand times."

"You haven't told me for a long time. I'll start and you finish," she said, as if making a concession. "Papa told you Sagrario had to sleep in your room because you were about to have a brother. And she told you it would be better if this brother wouldn't be born."

I sighed. "I was ten, and Sagrario was a year younger. Then Papa told Sagrario and me, 'This afternoon we're moving Sagrario's bed to your room.' Sagrario said, 'Why? I like my room.' And Papa answered, 'Because you're going to have a brother and he's going to need a lot of space.' He left happy. Sagrario looked at me and said, 'I wish he wouldn't be born.' We were playing with beautiful dolls our aunt gave us, they had real hair. Sagrario could still walk, though barely. And I asked, 'Why?' She answered, 'Because I'll be cured if he dies.' 'Why do you believe that?' I asked. And she told me, 'Because that's the way it is. Everybody says people don't have two sick kids in one family. So if he's sick, I'll be fine.' And I said, 'Then I want him to die too.' But you were born, you were healthy, and you grabbed everyone's finger with your tiny hands. And Sagrario said, 'Now I'm going to die.' 'No, you're not going to die,' I told her. 'Because I'm always with you and I won't let the ghosts take you away.' 'I'm going to die alone one night, no one will notice, and you won't be able to do anything,' she said. 'Yes, I can,' I promised her. 'I'll be with you when you die and I'll tell them to take me.' And she said, 'No, you won't.'"

"But you weren't there," said Nena. "Sagrario died alone."

"Yes," I answered. "We found her alone in the morning. As soon as I promised her I would let the ghosts take me instead of her, I started having nightmares. Dark spirits were all around me and I couldn't sleep. I cried so much Papa made Sagrario tell what was going on. She told him everything and he punished us hard. Then that night, before we fell asleep, Sagrario talked to me. 'They don't need to take you instead of me,' she said. 'It's not necessary.'"

My mother came into the bedroom. She had adjusted Sagrario's three dresses to my size and folded them with care.

"What were you talking about?" she asked.

Nena dashed into the hallway.

"Nothing!" she shouted as she ran away.

My mother shook her head.

"I don't want you talking to her anymore about death, or Sagrario, or ghosts in the shadows. She's obsessed with death and it's not normal for a girl of her age. This summer I'm going to invite some of her friends to make the house cheerful. She should watch more TV and ask for toys for Christmas instead of…." After a pause she continued, "I've been thinking, you could take your herbarium with you. The country house isn't like a city house. The nearest town is far away, and you need something to keep you busy. It's a good place to work on your collection."

"But it's so hard to carry," I protested. "Besides, they don't want me to bring toys."

"No, it's not. And it was your aunt who gave you your first flower press."

She kept packing my clothes.

"The house was yours too, wasn't it?" I asked suddenly.

"Yes, I sold it along with everything in it."

"Why did you sell your share of the inheritance?"

My mother didn't answer right away. When she spoke again, her voice was different.

"Because we needed money." Then she turned away. "Natalia, I heard you crying last night. Were you having nightmares again?"

"Yes," I said.

"The turtle?"

"Yes."

"They don't have animals anymore. You won't see any. You're not going to have nightmares there."

I nodded and went to my room. I threw myself onto Sagrario's bed. It felt strange to be lying there, on her bed that was now mine, after I had shared the room with Nena during the last year. My life had been constant moving from one room to another.

There were some changes. The small television, which nobody watched, a few old issues of teen magazines, two large black and white oxygen tanks, the ones we hadn't got rid of, which flanked the bed like canopy columns.

I got up. It was going to be a hot day. I opened the balcony window. It was the only room away from the street and the traffic noise, and that's why Sagrario used it. From there I saw a park that was built five years earlier, with green benches, pigeons, and a fountain. Grandparents were sitting there and having lunch with their grandchildren. Sagrario had enjoyed looking out at the park and imagining what their lives were like.

Then a boy slightly older than me appeared. Under his arm he held a blue folder and a book. He sat on a bench in front of our window and opened his book. I watched him with interest. He read for a half hour. Then he got up, straightened his pants, and left. I stuck my head out the window to watch him until he disappeared around the corner, swallowed up in traffic. "That's him," I thought. Sagrario's love. Every morning she had waited for him and watched him, and he didn't know and never even once looked toward the balcony. Love lurks in strange places. I threw myself onto the bed again. "Now he's mine," I thought, surprised by the unexpected gift my sister had left me.

I packed my luggage, wrapped the tools for my herbarium as if they were treasures, and listened to my parents' advice. Nena made me another drawing for the trip. It was a field sown with flowers and crosses. I hid it from my mother.

"Be careful with poisonous plants," Nena said as she hugged me tight, turning her chubby knuckles white.

"Don't worry."

"Is Sagrario going with you?"

"Yes," I said, touching her nose with the tip of my index finger. "Like always. I'll take Sagrario with me."

It was a scorching day, the damp stuck to our skin. It was a prelude to the warm, pleasant summer, which I didn't imagine when I left my house that morning. I remembered each step along the path that had grown old and recognized little by little the memories we had left behind.

There was a house in the middle of the field, surrounded by flowers, water, dark trees, and running children, and a grandmother with amethyst necklaces and coral cameos, and a grandfather with a silver cane. A little fairy tale cottage where the girls were dressed in long gowns and added a pearl to their necklaces each year. And they hosted balls where they slid across the marble floor, their dresses rustling, feather fans in their hands.

At least that's what the grown-ups who told the stories assured us, and that's what my mother said, too, bringing back from oblivion what her grandparents and their grandparents had passed on to her, long after the dresses, feathers, and laughter behind the fans had faded, because none of us, not even my mother nor my aunt, had lived through those splendid days, and you couldn't tell what had really happened from what had been made up each time those stories were told.

That evening I left the village, which was solitary and somber as a funeral. The streetlamps ended barely one kilometer out of the village, and the road was lit by a few yellow lights on old walls. Even though it had been a sunny day, streams of water ran through the street, and I supposed it had rained. A few scattered sheep were looking for shelter and bleating under the black trees. The woods became thicker. When I was little, I imagined that the branches sticking into the sky were goblins' arms trying to snatch me away. I closed my eyes and thought about Sagrario. Somewhere on this earth, she raised her feeble arms, petrified in an oak tree.

It was my first time to go to the country all by myself, but I didn't think of that until much later. As I pressed my forehead against the cold window, it struck me that I had already lived through this. During most of my trip, I knew all my movements in advance, as if a strange vision was telling me what would come next. It was just like those dreams that turned into nightmares, and I was afraid everything was the turtle's trick to seize me while I slept. I said my name seven times, and the strange feeling began to lift. I opened my eyes again and found myself on the way to the country house.

My cousins had been there for days when I arrived. They greeted me outside the house, under the rose bushes that arched over the door. It had been three years since I'd last seen them, and still confused by Sagrario's breath in the oak trees, the heat, the night falling upon us, I noticed only that Roberto was much taller than me and that Irlanda's smile was beautiful in the last rays of the afternoon sun.

Time does foolish things suddenly. It starts running, or it stops. There was a time when I had blind faith in the clock. Hours ticked away at their own pace, faster in my house, slower when I was in school, but the grains of sand kept falling, which made me grow, measured with both clock hands.

Time started to play tricks on me when the minutes of greetings and kisses from my cousins stretched into eternity, when Irlanda's sideways glance seemed frozen in the air, or when my hands, which had never been clumsy before, missed Roberto's. I suspected then that time goes round like the hands of a clock, and mine would have to go round and round, like a story that repeats forever, around the house and its green fields.

2

Sagrario must have been the large oak tree that stood at the end of the garden next to the house. She had loved that house more than any of us, and she often wrote in her diary about our childhood summers in the garden and the small hut we had built.

> *Sometimes when my heart feels like a hollow stone in my chest, I think about those carefree days six or seven years ago, when N. and I sneaked out to the meadow during siesta and hid from Grandmother until it grew dark and suddenly we became alarmed. The floorboard on the ground was ajar, and the grass rotted underneath, and we had to pull it out and put down the boards again. It seems impossible to me now, but I used to be able to walk to the meadow or sometimes climb a tree. I'm crying, but I feel my heart beating again.*

I imagined her buried under the oak tree, with the grass growing over her, far from the coldness of the cemetery where the flowers withered under the first rays of the sun. We had made a mistake. But that place wasn't ours anymore, and my sister wouldn't have liked to be staying forever on someone else's land.

When we were very young and it was story time, we learned that the house had been the pride of the village at the beginning of the last century, and we had to look haughty and keep our backs straight before the envious eyes of the villagers, just as the house stood straight and arrogant despite its decrepitude.

Everything was arranged beforehand—our places at the table, the gifts for the grandchildren, the dirty and clean clothes. We waited for Grandmother to start eating first, then joined her. We weren't allowed to leave the table, whisper, or leave food on our plates. Nor were we allowed to talk loudly, run around the house, or move objects from where they belonged. Grandmother kept us under control with her prying eyes, and flew into a rage when we dirtied something. Before bed, she went around the house with a rag to clean all the things that could have been dirtied—the door handles, the liquor glasses, or the pear-shaped light bulbs, which hung next to the bed like strange black eggs.

When we drove into town, Sagrario sat in the middle of the back seat, farthest from the windows, because, as I learned later, Grandmother had done her best to keep anyone from knowing that her granddaughter was dying like the walls of a worm-eaten house. The whole village had always hated us.

"I don't know why they hate us," Sagrario said, enveloped in the smell of medicine in her airless room, during the last days of May.

I had stopped reading aloud to Sagrario, who didn't sleep anymore, and she sat up against the pillows.

"Not dancing ever again, not knowing what lies outside my window, an empty space or this half-remembered city, not waking up ever again, not imagining myself sleeping." She wept slow tears and murmured. "I want to go now. I want it to be over once and for all. I'm ready to die right now. I must die now that I stray from the only path I've known, the only one I've been allowed to take. And I walk alone…."

I gave her a long stare and could hear the silence left by her death. Then I laid her tired head gently down on her pillow and let her sleep until the next day. In the morning we found her dead, so far down the path that she barely waved us goodbye.

Still, it's true they hated us, and her daughters' marriages, which deeply disappointed Grandmother, hadn't freed us from their silent rage. Stories still circulated about beautiful Hibernia, about an ancestor who healed by touch, and about his son, a playboy with burning eyes who seduced the young girls in the village and lured them into the woods with false promises. The villagers would have paid anything to see the country house finally empty.

It was an elongated, solid building. There were the stables on one side, the barn on the other. However, the rectangular shape gave the impression of slenderness because of the galleries with high arches and the tower that stood high above the rest of the house and grazed the power lines. It had been designed as a summerhouse, and the glass gallery formed the longest wall of the main living room. The bedrooms that faced south and west also had galleries. The windows remained intact, but the tower and chapel, with their medieval facades, stood crumbling, crawling with vermin.

"You keep an eye on Mama," Sagrario had told me, "because she's going to sell her inheritance piece by piece, as she has started to do, and the rest of the family, leeches that they are, will take advantage of her. They may fool Mama, but don't let them fool you. We'll end up with nothing and that'll be the end of us." She continued, her eyes closed. "Don't think that I'm talking about the way our aunt and uncle have treated us. I have no hard feelings against them now. I'm saying this for you two, Nena and you, because I'm not going to be around much longer."

My uncle, a skinny man who never grew old and had grown up in the city, leased the land to the distrustful people in the village. When I arrived, he was ending the meeting in the barn in which he wanted to sell the land. They hadn't reached an agreement, because the price he was asking seemed very high. But he knew they would give in.

"They wanted this house, but they won't get it. It's worth more than they could pay. If they want the farms, they have to pay what they're worth. 'There's more to life than money,' one of them said. And I told him, 'What else is there? I have to make a living too, and money doesn't grow on trees.'"

I imagined the villagers looting the house, breaking the stained-glass gallery windows and filling up the well with stones, until the house became a ghostly ruin that gathered darkness on moonless nights. The children would sneak out to visit the house and whisper to each other that it was haunted.

"The sale is almost final. The details still have to be worked out, and I need to see money. Without that, there's no deal."

With deals like these, he had become rich. For twenty years he had managed a small shop he had started. With the savings he put together, he had bought houses, land, abandoned plots. He waited patiently for the right moment to resell them, then reaped ever greater profits, without losing sight of the previous ones.

My parents didn't talk much about him. At family gatherings, my father was left out, shy and quiet while my uncle spoke. He was a draftsman, not a businessman. My uncle couldn't sit still, talked loudly, and had the shrewdness that was lacking in my family, who had never learned how to make money. His gifts were always unusual and surprising, wrapped in boxes that seemed too luxurious for the toys inside and we reused the boxes to wrap our own gifts.

Whenever we returned home, my father would close himself off in the corner between the windows where he had his drawing board and computer, and spend more time on his drawings than usual. We were allowed to use the computer, but I didn't like feeding my ideas into a machine that swallowed them, and I preferred to hand in my homework typed on my old typewriter.

My aunt embraced me, introduced me to everyone, then asked about everyone in the family, with not-quite convincing enthusiasm.

"And Nena? Why didn't you bring her along?"

I changed the subject. Silence stretched between us as we thought of Sagrario. My aunt didn't ask about her as she had done before. She reacted immediately. She handed me sheets and a can of bug spray.

"Irlanda cleaned the room facing the well for you. She sleeps with her friends in the room with the gallery, but because you don't know each other, I thought you would feel awkward, at least at first. When you make friends, you can sleep in their room, or move to the one you like best."

"I'd be delighted to have you sleep in my room," said Irlanda, "but if someone else joins us, the room will be so crowded."

Years ago Irlanda stole two red apples from Sagrario and me, caramel apples Grandmother had bought in town one Saturday—one for each grandchild. Irlanda ate hers in the car, and Sagrario and I kept ours on a plate in the pantry. By dinnertime they had disappeared, but I saw that my cousin's jacket was sticky with caramel. We didn't tell on her, but since then Sagrario had held a grudge against her.

"The four of you could sleep on mattresses on the floor," said Roberto. "But you're a sleepyhead, and you'd do anything to keep your bed."

"He says so because I take a siesta to recover my strength, while he'd rather go out to set traps for poor animals and wear himself out running around in the woods like a savage," Irlanda explained to me.

"Irlanda gets up late. Then she lies down for a couple hours, and then when she isn't sleepy at night, she's in no hurry to go to bed. Of course, she's in no hurry to get up either. We let her do that now because she's on vacation," said my aunt, hugging Irlanda against her chest. "And because she knows how to stretch the hours to do what she has to do."

"And your luggage, Natalia?" my uncle asked. "What do you want us to do with it?"

I followed him to the hallway and pulled out my clothes and the small gifts I brought.

"I have my flower press and herbarium sheets in this bag," I said. "They need to be in some place dry."

"I'll leave them in the barn for now." He picked them up and dropped them. "What are they made of? Lead? Go into the kitchen. It's cool out here."

The leaves danced in the wind, and showed their pale bellies, as if embarrassed, outside the windows. The summer heat lingered in the air, much too hot for June. I opened and closed my fists and looked at my life lines—they were damp with sweat.

"Well," said my aunt. "Everyone back home is doing well."

"Yes," I answered, distracted. With each new gust of wind, the leaves spun and twirled, turning pale with fear.

"Come on. Don't be standing in the middle of the kitchen. Don't be shy. Go sit with them and ask them to cook something for you. You disappoint me, girls. Can't you give Natalia a proper welcome?"

My cousins' friends had remained a little apart. They never stopped smiling, and my aunt spoke to them as if they were her own children. They were playing chess. Then I remembered suddenly, and I got up and handed them the gifts from my mother. A gauze scarf for my aunt, slippers for my uncle, a penknife for Roberto, and a bottle of perfume for Irlanda.

"It's beautiful," my aunt said, wrapping the scarf around her neck. "Always so considerate. I don't know how she could still feel like giving gifts."

Irlanda let her girlfriends smell the perfume. I breathed more easily. They hadn't recognized the boxes that contained the stuffed animals from three years ago. My mother wasn't very careful, and I never knew how my aunt and uncle would react. I imagined them setting aside a room for the boxes and gifts they gave, our forgotten boxes among them. My uncle returned after a while.

"The barn was closed, so I left them in the tower. When you go fetch them, be careful. Ask Roberto to go with you. You'll be fine, but when you go down the stairs, you could slip and fall. Who's got the key to the barn? If you lose any of the keys, I'll skin you alive."

"I never lose anything," said Irlanda. "Are you staying for dinner?"

"No, honey. If we don't leave now, imagine how late we'll get home. Need anything? Do you have enough food, enough money?"

"What else do they need? They have water and light," said my uncle.

"And nothing else," said Roberto.

"You don't need anything else. Well water is better than tap water. It doesn't cost you anything to take out a couple of buckets. You shouldn't get used to luxuries. Soon you'll forget how to open a door for yourselves."

"He's grumpy," my aunt said, pretending to confide in me. "But he has a heart of gold. You have the phone number? Do you need money?"

"What for?" Irlanda asked, exasperated. "Where do you expect us to go shopping? Go now."

My uncle gave Roberto and his friend other instructions. They planned how to cut down the weeds around the house.

The main road would soon reach one of his farms, and my uncle intended to keep the house until then. Then my aunt and uncle told the boys to be sensible and take care of us girls. When they said goodbye, it was already pitch black.

"I'll come back tomorrow and see how you're doing," my aunt said, kissing Irlanda. "Behave yourselves."

We heard them leaving. They returned a moment later, because they had forgotten to leave food for Irlanda's cat, a formidable cat with long, bluish fur that had been sleeping in the living room.

"He's a very nice cat," my aunt assured me, piling the cans of meat on top of each other. We were going to leave him home with us, but your uncle and I plan to go away for a couple of weeks, and he'll have to stay here anyway. Besides, Irlanda is very fond of him."

She stroked the cat's back. *Watch them close because they're going to sell the inheritance, as they have started to do, and we'll end up with nothing, we're not going to last very long.* My aunt looked at me, smiling, and said one last goodbye before they left. I watched the cat for a moment. He blinked from time to time, filled with calm. "No," I thought, "he has nothing to do with a turtle."

While I was sitting at the table for the second time, a new feeling came over me, a pang of unease I tried to dispel. A knot in my stomach gave me a strange, moving sensation, the sensation that my life had not been like this, that there was something I needed to win back, something was slowly slipping away before I knew it. Then I turned and found myself with my cousins and their friends around the chessboard. That's how the summer began.

3

*I*rlanda was more beautiful than I remembered. As a girl her angelic face had been marred by only two defects—her thin light hair and almost always elusive eyes. But now her hair was nicely done, and she had learned to look out from under her lashes.

Until three years earlier we had spent a lot of time together. Then she was sent to an international school. My sisters and I were always told to be like her. Even when she played with clay, she kept herself clean and neat, and that pleased Grandmother. She knew the right thing to say at the right time, and had a way of getting whatever she wanted from grown-ups with smiles. Irlanda was wonderful and graceful. We didn't look at all like cousins.

I barely knew Roberto. He was too old for my sisters and me. Their friends, one boy and two girls, went to the same school. One girl was a brunette and the other a blonde with shockingly light hair. The boy had a far-off look in his eyes. The friends were kind but distant, having been told probably what certain subjects they shouldn't bring up with me.

The blonde had left the chessboard and followed Irlanda into the kitchen, taking out the plates and napkins for dinner. From time to time she put her arm around Irlanda's waist and behaved as if they were the only ones in the room. I'd never had girlfriends. I didn't need them. Once I had played on the beach with a girl who let me borrow her bucket and shovel, and we jumped over the waves together. But I never saw her again.

Sagrario was with me in school and at home, and when she couldn't go to school anymore, Nena and I went straight home slipping through the gaps between cars, to keep her company and tell her what happened in the outside world. That was what our parents told us to do, and they were never wrong.

I had been a mischievous girl with a strong imagination, and I was always getting Sagrario into trouble. She loyally followed me, even though she was more thoughtful and less impulsive and always warned me of disaster.

"We'll be in trouble," she'd say. Then, helpless before the inevitable, she would shrug and add, "Oh well. You're the oldest."

The girls around me cared only about their studies or their parents or both, and none of them shared my interests. None of them had discovered the pleasure of obeying grown-ups and the satisfaction of a job well done. All were in love with singers and actors and adorned their books with their photos, and read teen magazines for instructions for putting on lipstick. They weren't like my bright little sister or Sagrario.

Now Sagrario was gone, and I didn't know anyone my age. When Nena wasn't playing near me, I was so alone that I sometimes talked aloud to feel a voice around me. Irlanda asked if I had already had dinner, and put a fruit bowl and a small jug of white roses in front of me.

"You still like flowers?"

I smiled. "I brought my herbarium with me."

"Good. There's nothing here. No television, no people, not even books. If you get bored easily, you go crazy."

"I don't get bored easily."

"We won't let you get bored," said Roberto's friend, speaking for the first time.

"No," said Roberto. "There's always excitement. Like when you're sleeping, you feel something on you and it's a rat running across your bed."

The girls protested in chorus.

"Or bedbugs," he continued. "You don't notice them until they're all over you."

"Don't be so childish!" Irlanda said. "By the way, Roberto, do you remember my friend, the brunette with an upturned nose, the one you chased all over the dance floor and who had enough sense to snub you?"

"Yes."

"You won't see her at school this year."

The blonde opened her mouth wide.

"No! What happened?"

"Early Sunday morning she got caught with three grams of cocaine in her pocket. She had spent the night with a boy in a hotel. She said the drugs belonged to the friend she had gone to visit, and it turned out to be true, but she's not coming back to school in the fall."

"Did she get expelled?"

"No," said Irlanda. "I didn't say that. She'd rather change schools. I don't think anyone would dare come back under those circumstances."

"Nowadays, nobody would be surprised that she's going with a boy. Besides, who hasn't dreamed of spending a weekend like that?"

"But everyone would talk about it. She wouldn't be able to stop the whole school from talking, and she'd have a hard time talking to us," explained the blonde, with a trace of envy in her voice. "I wouldn't be speaking to her."

"You must follow certain rules of conduct if you want to mix with decent people. If you want to have a good time and live on the edge, you should do it discreetly."

"Somebody must have reported her," said Roberto's friend. "Principals don't spy on students during the summer to try to dig up dirt on them. Somebody must have been jealous of her."

"You saw her that same day, right, Irlanda?"

"Yes. The same afternoon I saw her on the street, near my house, where I had agreed to meet my friends. I said hello to her, but she looked away. We never got along well, we weren't close friends, but that's no excuse for snubbing me. After all, the scandal didn't do her any harm."

We talked a bit more. I was very tired, but if I found a rat or a spider on my bed, I would have screamed until I lost my voice, and I could never stand making a fool of myself in front of my cousins' prep-school friends.

"If I stay here longer, I think I'll fall asleep at the table," I said, trying to appear awake, even though my smile wasn't all that sincere. "I'm having fun, but I'd better go to bed."

Irlanda accompanied me to the stairs, helped me make the bed, and closed the shutters.

"Don't pay any attention to Roberto. He just wanted to tease us. There aren't any rats or anything like that. We put out traps and poison more than a month ago, and there are no more rats."

"It doesn't matter," I said. "As a last resort, we have the cat."

"The cat? He's so spoiled with the cow's liver and treats we give him. He wouldn't even notice rats. We fumigated the whole place, so there aren't any bugs left." We smoothed out the sheets. "Now you know where we are. Roberto sleeps in his usual place, and Gabriel in the other room. The red room is also clean, but I thought you would rather sleep here."

Sagrario and I had always slept in the red room, the two of us together in the same bed, with sheets so tight that we couldn't even move our arms. *Aren't you cold? Or is it just me? My feet are always cold. Don't move. There... now let's pretend we're asleep. Are you asleep, Natalia? Are you asleep?* I shook my head. Irlanda smoothed the folds in the bedspread.

"I was counting the days until you would come," she said. "The house didn't seem complete without you. It feels strange to go back to places where you grew up. Don't you think? Don't you miss Grandma? I can almost hear her voice. She would have been pleased to see us so grown-up and sensible," she sighed. "There's a time when you think you'll never grow up and grownups will be always right. Then you grow up without realizing it, and all the rooms that seemed enormous before have shrunk."

I was thinking that grown-ups would always be right, and that growing up was terribly slow and painful, but Irlanda leaned over the bed with so much grace that there was no doubt she had grown up. And the realization hurt me, which somehow made me grow up too.

"I don't want to grow up," I mumbled.

"Don't be silly. When you grow up, you're allowed to do anything you want."

"But only children are allowed to make mistakes."

Irlanda looked at me, a bit surprised.

"Do you remember this room? Grandmother spent so many hours here, sipping coffee and praying for everyone in the family, both the living and dead. When she was very old, her bed was brought in here, and she hardly left the room, poor Grandma. Of course, you may not remember. I've spent more time here than you."

Wearing a dress and a ribbon in her fluffed-up hair, Irlanda had spent whole afternoons seated next to Grandmother, when they were out on their visits. At night we heard them coming back, Irlanda almost overcome by sleep, Grandmother proud but also tired. We gave her a kiss before going to bed, making sure that we had washed our hands and face, because she would notice, with her clear eyes, if we hadn't done so.

"I'm so glad you're here," she said again before she left. I turned my face toward the wall, not knowing what to say. "Good night."

I couldn't fall asleep right away. My bed sagged in the middle, inexplicably soft, and the bug spray smell made me sneeze. I tried to think of the boy I had met that morning, his book, the bench, the park beyond him, but I got distracted right away. I heard the others going to bed. They went upstairs one by one, tiptoeing over the creaky wooden floors. When the last door was shut, silence fell over the house, and Sagrario, drawn by the chemical smell, appeared in the other bed in my room, as she looked in her last days, when the smell of medicine had filled the air and the cool May wind kept us from opening the window to let in fresh air.

I was sitting next to her and reading aloud to keep her distracted. I had taken my mother's place, because it was going to be a long night and Sagrario hardly slept. She sat up against her pillows.

"It's horrible to have only one life to live, and my life has been like this!" she said in a hoarse voice. "It's horrible to go on living like this while my memories do me no good, and to feel the seconds fly by and not to be able do anything. I keep looking at the clock, and it doesn't stop, and death will end my time. It's horrible not to be able to dance, not to have danced!"

She would get quiet and then start complaining again.

"Not to visit other countries, not knowing what spreads beyond the corners of the park, an empty space or a half-remembered city, not feeling any more kisses than the ones I have already received, not meeting other people, not knowing what you'll say about me, not seeing Nena grow up, not waking up again, not feeling that I sleep." She cried big tears like hailstones. "I'm ready to die now. I want to leave this place. I want my time to end once and for all. I want to be free from sadness and free from the fear of night in another world. I must die, now that I see the beginning of the path, and I'm on it without fear. A path I'm walking alone...."

I looked at her for a long time and could hear the silence her death was leaving behind. I placed the pillows under her head and let her sleep and slip into her new world. We found her dead in the morning, her heart stopped, her mouth half open.

The wind started lashing the windows, seeping through the cracks under the doors, and I found myself in the room with a view of the well, alone again, not knowing if I was dreaming or if time was coiling around itself. Did I have to relive the same chain of events since Sagrario's burial and come to the country house and sleep in the room facing the well and remember Sagrario on her deathbed and her funeral, like looking into facing mirrors, reflecting each other into infinity. But I stayed still. I gradually remembered there were new things, things that I hadn't lived through, and time marched on, like it was supposed to.

I ducked under the sheets and listened, my heart pounding against my chest. The wind slipped through the fingers of the dead and carried their voices to me. I didn't want to listen anymore. If I could make out what they were whispering, they would force me to join them, and I would remain captive forever, imprisoned between two worlds.

In those moments, the night split open to reveal the path where the two worlds met. If I could get up and draw a circle around the place I was sleeping, I would be safe, but it was very dark, the moon had come out, and the ghosts could snatch me if I unwrapped myself from my cocoon of blankets. I shut my eyes tight, trying not to think of the turtle. It wasn't the first time it followed me to the country house, and I prayed Sagrario would hold it back, dancing among the new spirits.

I woke up and found myself in an unfamiliar room. The day had dawned. I opened the shutters and glanced toward the west in the early-morning sky. The sunlight reached the rest of the house much later, and I could see the shadows disappear with their burden of fears. The sun quickly rose over the field. The well bucket, which was still used, had rolled across the grass.

Years ago, a small orchard grew there, but now there were only rows of red dirt, hardened among the nettles, a multicolored jumble of wild plants and brambles, and farther away, woods of chestnut and bay trees. We weren't allowed to go that far. We plucked bay leaves from the shrubs growing next to the wall of our house and added them to our food. One red cabbage survived in the old orchard, with its bleeding heart, next to the stubborn chamomile bushes and stones that had crumbled off the boundary wall.

Things reverted to their normal forms in the daylight, and there was nothing to be scared of. The dream shook the dust off its wings, and only those creatures who lived among dirt and cobwebs still lay asleep. *Are you asleep, Natalia? Are you sleeping?*

I looked at my room. I had never been crazy about it, because it never got enough sunlight and it was cluttered with old junk that Grandmother didn't allow us to touch. But now there were only a wide bed, a closet with a cloudy mirror, and a crucifix hung above the bed. The furniture was ornate, but it seemed lost in the void. The walls were bare, with dark marks left by other furniture and at least two other crosses that used to hang on them. I remembered a few high-backed chairs of woven esparto-grass, and a small tea table where our knees banged.

Don't run down the hallways, Natalia. Don't play with the figurines.

Don't touch the table. Don't you see you're making it dirty? Why don't you go sit and read a story, like your sister?

Come on, Natalia. Let's read a story together and play princesses. Let's make tiaras out of silver paper and go slay dragons and stepmothers.

The sun was already high. I got dressed without any noise, finally happy that I had decided to be away from my parents. Sagrario would be happy to dance among the tall grass, to forget her bed, pillows, and the sadness of not being able to tell the difference between sleep and wakefulness. It was going to be a gorgeous day, the summer stretched before us, and the ghosts had stayed behind.

4

*I*rlanda was still asleep, but Roberto was already up and told me to have a big breakfast. He wanted to study engineering, but always said he had a farmer's soul. He liked to walk the fields, measure and mark, and fix things up. From the time he was very young, his father had taken him to the workshop and taught him to value manual labor and to never take pride in being lazy. On his hand he had traces of a splinter wound. He was smoking his second cigarette of the day, and I waved off the smoke. Smiling, he warned me about the hard work ahead of us.

"The girls thought it would take only one day to clean the house, but the dust settles constantly, red dust like field dirt, which stains everything, and there's no way to remove it."

He left whistling, biting an apple so green that it made me shiver. Irlanda's cat lay down in the sun, his eyes half closed, and I made a detour to avoid stepping on him. He looked up, his drowsy eyes following my shadow, and went back to dozing. My steps echoed through the living room. A magpie perched on a tree and shrieked. Then it flew to the power line and alighted next to three other black birds. The midday sun would dry the grass, but it was still wet with dew. Roberto waited for his friend at the gate. After a while he appeared on the hill, and they disappeared from sight.

Irlanda gave me some old clothes to wear and divided the chores among us. Roberto was right. As we cleaned the living room, dust covered our smocks and got into our hair. All the rooms were tapestried with cloth, and we had to rub the walls little by little, barely making them wet with foam. The sunlight from the gallery had bleached the wine-red, almost violet color of the living room. It was a slow, endless task, and one that awakened memories of the past. The muffled voices behind the fans remained in the tapestries and mixed with new noises.

My cousin's girlfriends chatted nonstop. At times they included me in their conversation. They talked about people I didn't know and places I'd never been, but I enjoyed listening to them. It felt so pleasant to chase the morning sun, with its thread of dust floating through the light, and it felt so simple to be young in an old house and to join in the chatter and laughter that I took deep breaths and filled my lungs with fresh air, with those unfamiliar names the girls gossiped about.

Their school had held a prom last spring. The girls had dressed in long gowns, and the boys, like chivalrous knights, had asked them to dance while slow music was played. Some boys were worth it, and others weren't. They mentioned a boy named Armando, who made them sigh and had worn a white rose. But they were resigned that he had eyes only for Irlanda. Then, completely apart, as far away from the girls as distant stars, there were the older boys like Roberto and his friends. The men.

At my school we organized parties on Christmas and toward

the end of the school year the students recited poems and staged short plays. The parents gave enthusiastic rounds of applause and took photos of their children when they received glittering trophies and diplomas.

The brunette stayed quiet and complied with Irlanda's wishes. She seemed submissive body and soul to Irlanda. The blonde was obliging, almost subservient. She cooed at the cat as she stroked him and made expansive gestures as she spoke. My cousin pretended not to listen. Her portrait-like face tilted toward the floor so gracefully that she appeared to have nothing in common with her girlfriends, also beautiful, but so ordinary. She piled books on the floor, then spread them out in the sun on the stone benches in the garden. The pages curled up at the edges, as if complaining about the treatment they received.

"There are some very old books," said Irlanda. "And two interesting German editions."

"Irlanda loves antiques. I think she should be an artist," the blonde murmured to me, but it was still loud enough for Irlanda to hear. "Do you see those prayer books? With gold leaf and varnish, she can do wonders."

Whenever we visited the house, Grandfather took Sagrario to the library in the attic. He would take me out to the garden and teach me the names of plants and let Irlanda have an afternoon snack with the grown-ups in the living room. Irlanda had grown up, which meant I too was growing up, and Sagrario had been left quiet and small in her grave. I brushed an old tapestry and tried to think about something else.

The girls kept on talking about their world.

"After the prom, I was surprised your brother didn't invite Armando to spend the summer vacation with us. He seemed totally crazy about you."

Irlanda smiled. "Did you think I would let a boy like that live with me in a house for three months without grown-ups?"

"A boy like that? What do you mean? What's wrong with him? Irlanda, Armando is perfect."

"That's what's wrong," she said, winking at me. I smiled back at her. "My parents aren't blind."

"When are we old enough to be independent from our parents? Someday I'll go on vacation with anyone I want, and I'll do anything I want. Anyway, we'd have a lot more fun without Gabriel," said the blonde. "He's so reserved...."

"I was afraid an older boy wouldn't want to be locked up here, where there's nothing more than fields and sky, and I was glad he agreed to come. But please," continued Irlanda, with a look of disdain on her face, "Gabriel is completely stupid. When he opens his mouth and says his name, he's got nothing left to say."

The blonde laughed, obliging.

"You're so right. But he's loaded with money. And he's not bad looking. He isn't like your brother, of course, but he isn't bad looking."

"No," said Irlanda. "He's not bad looking at all. He has a nice face and beautiful eyes."

"He has demented eyes," I said.

We ate seated on the grass because the table in the living room stank of varnish, and the sunlight had thinned out. The sky was so clear and so blue that it would have been a shame to go inside. Irlanda tied her hair with a white ribbon and sat next to me.

"Are you happy here?"

I nodded. She was so lovely with her angelic smile and her white ribbon that I was sorry not to have seen her surrounded by handsome boys at one of the dances. I wished her girlfriends would leave us alone so that I could talk to her and ask her if she remembered the other times when we had eaten under the same apple tree in the garden, or the times when we sneaked out to the meadow with Sagrario to play in the small hut. All that didn't fit in with the dances and Armando with his white rose.

"Very happy."

"I want us to always stay like this, as happy as we are now."

Irlanda squeezed my hand. She took charge of our food and house with the same grace when she placed refined sheets of gold leaf on the old prayer books or cleaned the columns of a complicated engraving with a feather duster. She had the gift of making everything look easy.

My aunt came to check on us that afternoon and got upset when she saw how we washed curtains.

"You girls today have no common sense. You're not supposed to clean these with foam and spray, but with water, soap, and elbow grease," she said and sent us outside while she took over the task, and the cat, who was prowling around, gave us a wicked look.

Irlanda made a charming grimace, took an old bedspread, and carefully spread it over the grass. She fell asleep under the apple tree, covering her face with her forearm, enveloped in the folds of the silky bedspread, and I sat next to her, her head on my lap, to watch over her while she slept and not let anything disturb her sleep. The leaves of the tree showed their pale bellies, and I wanted to dry a few leaves from the branches.

I heard the echo of distant blows, which the afternoon soaked up like a sponge, and I looked up. I didn't want to sleep before drawing a circle around us, but there was nothing but grass within my reach. Irlanda's girlfriends had joined us under the shadow of the tree and were dozing. I carefully placed Irlanda's head down on the bedspread and caressed her hair.

I walked to the old chapel and pulled out a small branch from the shrubs. I stepped on shards of colored glass from the stained-glass windows. Years ago they had painted chubby cherubs on the cornices. I stood on tiptoe and peeked through a broken window. There remained several dismantled kneeling benches and a statue in the niche. Roberto was still outside the house. He had inspected the small tower and reinforced some areas with Gabriel. I went around the chapel and approached the tower. I went to the stairs where the boys were working. I saw them hammering and drilling, their faces flushed, and I went up to them.

"Do you want me to bring you anything?" I asked. "I have nothing to do."

"Water, Natalia, please," said Roberto. "I'm dying of thirst."

I went down to the well, filled a bottle with water, and brought it to the tower. The boys stopped, wiped their foreheads, and gulped down the water.

"Does it hurt?" I asked Roberto, pointing at the scar on his hand.

"No. It's nothing."

"Your dad left my herbarium stuff over there," I said. "Are they in your way?"

"No."

I arranged the herbarium sheets with care and set them on the flower press. Then Irlanda came looking for me.

"What are you doing up there?"

Her voice startled me, but my cousin was all smiles, as always.

"I'm fixing my flower press," I said. "The herbarium sheets weren't set properly."

"Let the boys do that. Let's go. We shouldn't be here."

I saw her silhouette against the light, outlined against the brightness, and I thought this was exactly the place where we should be, an undetermined place between heaven and earth, like angels. "And like demons," I said to myself and went down the stairs. Her girlfriends had bright red cheeks, and their eyes reproached me for having abandoned my vigil over Irlanda's sleep. I felt obliged to talk about my flower press.

"Did you have to do it now?" asked the blonde.

I didn't answer, and no one said anything. They were still lying drowsy on the bedspread, but the magic had vanished. My aunt told us how to hang the curtains and which room each of them belonged to, and took me aside.

"Are you having a good time?"

"Yes."

"I'm glad. You weren't talking to Irlanda's girlfriends much. Don't be shy." Then she lowered her voice a little and spoke in an intimate tone. "Listen, try to make friends with them. They are girls of good family, and you can learn a lot from them. Listen to me. You know I love you. I want you to start meeting the right people. And if Irlanda gets cocky, don't mind her. She can be a bit bossy. Tell her she's only your cousin and don't let her bully you."

I promised to be friendly and not to let my cousin walk all over me, and we waved goodbye as she drove off. That night I stayed up very late with the girls in the kitchen. The two girlfriends formed a team and played chess against Irlanda, and they hardly spoke to me. I had time to think and reached the conclusion that they ignored me because I had dared go up the tower while the boys were there.

Irlanda came into my room before I went to bed.

"My girlfriends behaved like perfect fools," she said. "First, talking about the prom dance and then all that private conversation. The truth is, they are completely stupid. With Gabriel's dullness and their stupidity, they must have spoiled your dinner. But now you know. If you deal with people, this is the problem: you find yourself with people."

"They're very nice," I lied. "After all, not everyone has a chance to go to the prom."

"They talk about it as if it were really their social debut. It was really something simple. And it's not even our tradition, but it's my stupid school's custom, with its year-end dances and prom queens…. A lot of crap," she said with indifference. "They're a bit jealous of you. But the truth is, they're a bit jealous of everyone. They act like this when there are boys around. They're desperate to go out with a boy."

"I'm not interested in the boys. Besides, one of them is my cousin. How was I supposed to know the girls would get upset?" I stared at Irlanda and blurted out. "That nasty blonde kept staring at me all night, as if she might slap me."

"That nasty blonde is my mother's best friend's daughter and one of the most pampered girls I know. But I had to invite her because Mama adores her. Besides, she likes Roberto, and Roberto thinks she's not bad at all. She's not a bad person. She's just stupid." She looked at me and squeezed my arm. "Cheer up. They're not going to be here all summer. When they leave, we'll be comfortable here. If they pick on you again, just tell me. They'll listen to me. They always do what I tell them. That's what's good about stupid people. We're cousins, after all."

Something choked me in my throat, and I could almost taste the salty tears.

"I never thought you were like this, Irlanda," I said. "When we were young, sometimes you treated me so badly I wished you would go away." I wished she would end her visit or we could end ours, and especially, I wished she would die, strangled with one of the ribbons she used to wear in her hair.

Irlanda laughed. "That's a long time ago. Since then I've learned manners."

"Yes," I admitted. "You're a lady now."

"I'd rather be something more lively. A banker or a stockbroker," she said, wrinkling her nose. "At least they have power in their hands, and money. I don't want to wait for some kings to show up at my tower window. Open your eyes, Natalia. There's nothing better in the world than having power."

"Irlanda," I asked suddenly. "Do you remember Grandmother once bought us caramel apples, when we were young?"

"At the ice-cream stand, yes."

"Did you take ours? They were in the pantry."

"No," she said, already at the door. "Of course not."

That night, before I drifted off to sleep, I suddenly noticed that Sagrario hadn't appeared all day. I pretended to be happy for her, because I imagined her frolicking in the meadow, maybe playing with her turtle. But I couldn't deceive myself. I knew she was somewhere, wet and cold with the night dew, lost in the woods, or that Irlanda, dressed in white and light, kept her away. Two nights in a row no ghosts haunted my dreams, and I woke up, guilty and happy.

Despite my cousin's promise, her girlfriends weren't friendly toward me at all. They followed Irlanda everywhere she went and fawned over her like ladies-in-waiting. From then on, when I couldn't stand their whispers and couldn't breathe because my nose was clogged with dust, I went out into the fields and stayed there until it got dark, with an armful of herbs and flowers for my herbarium. The wheat was mixed with flowers, and heather and chicory grew in the road ditches, and my herbarium grew quickly. Almost every day I sat next to the well to write letters home, forcing a cheerful tone.

I wrote about whatever I was doing and described my cousin's girlfriends. I also talked about Irlanda and my aunt, because I knew my mother would want to hear about them. My baby sister sent me her drawings and once wrote me six lines in her large, round handwriting.

dear Natalia how are you I have many things to tell you it's sunny and I go to the cemetery every day sometimes I go to the beach with Silvia and it's sunny we catch fish Silvia's turtle died. I love you your Sister.

Silvia's turtle didn't worry me, because it had nothing to do with me, and at worst, by the time it reached the country house, the summer would be over and I would be gone. In my next letter, I included a note for her, also in large, simple letters so that she could read it.

It's a shame you didn't want to come, because it's a beautiful house. You've never been here, but I think you'd like it a lot. There's a very beautiful garden, and a tower with a princess locked up inside. Cousin Irlanda is very pretty, and Cousin Roberto is handsome, and they keep asking me about you. But because you didn't want to come, you're missing out on all the fun. I'm having a great time, and Sagrario enjoys herself living in the roots of every tree.

I thought for a moment and then crossed out the last sentence. My parents would read my letter to Nena and they wouldn't want me to tell her what Sagrario was doing.

I'm having a good time and can't wait to see you again. Be good and do what Mama and Papa tell you.

I missed Nena, but I felt only a slight longing, soft to the touch, some nights while I felt drowsy and watched the others play chess. Then I stared into the night outside the window, which reflected my image like a mirror, and I wondered what Nena was doing at that moment.

The house thrived and stretched day by day. I became fond of my room. I had put two tapestries on the walls and tulle curtains that wouldn't block the light from the west, which I later removed. The sun appeared outside the window, and the earth and green fields went mad with color. The shadows swelled, the magpies disappeared, scared away, letting the wind hiss among the power lines and the noises died down while the sun sank into the horizon.

Then the darkness swallowed the horizon, the ghosts of the

oaks and chestnuts brandished their claws trying to seize Sagrario, and the turtle crept toward my room. The turtle followed me, and I started running without looking back, trying to escape from its grasp, blindly, without knowing if it was still behind me or not, or if I had lived through this nightmare or it was my first dream and I had to wake up and live through everything again and again, endlessly. Someday I would get tired of running and the turtle would catch up with me.

I woke up with a tightness in my chest and ducked under the pillow until the daylight came in through the windows, and the light brought Irlanda's sweetness, Roberto's friendly concern, and Irlanda's girlfriends' malicious looks.

That's how another day slipped away. Near twilight, when the day's work was done, I went into the garden. The earth was bright red, and the sun had the same color over the hill. For a moment, I trembled, thinking about the approaching struggle between light and darkness, and I wanted to get up and run toward the house, so that the night wouldn't take me by surprise and seize the edge of my skirt and drag me to dance in the circle that the spirits form with the new ghosts. But then, just as I could see the shadows approaching, Irlanda called me and signaled from the window for me to come inside for dinner.

5

*I*rlanda was alone at the end of the month. Summoned by their parents, her girlfriends left. They were going to spend the rest of the summer in a white village by the sea, getting tanned in the constant whisper of waves, and the memory of the country house would become more intense as it faded into the distance, like love spells.

For a moment, I imagined the girls jumping over the waves with the girl who befriended me once, a long time ago, but they were much older than her, and they would complain because she splashed them while they bathed in the sun. Then my little friend suddenly morphed into a girl our age, and I tried to blink away the unpleasant image.

The two girls left the house in tears, hardly consoled by the idea that they would see Irlanda in the fall. The blonde flung her arms around Irlanda's neck and clung to her.

"Write me, and if you have a new dress made for the September dance, call me to tell me what it's like. Irlanda, write me every week. You won't forget, will you?"

The brunette, quiet and serious as usual, waited beside with her luggage. When Roberto closed the trunk and they went off, she suddenly straightened up, as if a heavy weight had been lifted from her shoulders. They had wanted only Roberto to take them, hoping, I imagined, that the occasion would give the blonde a chance to show her affection to him.

As a final gesture of goodwill, I had gathered flowers the night before so that they could take two bouquets as keepsakes. They were genuinely surprised and said goodbye to me more warmly than I had expected.

"But write me. Will you do that?"

Irlanda didn't seem much affected. She didn't make any fuss as she watched them leave. Nor did she say anything about the seaside village she herself might have wanted to visit. I was secretly happy. Those days I hoped for any sign that she was going to share her room with me, but she removed the mattresses her girlfriends had used and didn't say a word to me, so I continued to sleep in my room over the well. I was disappointed. A few days later I shyly hinted that I wanted to change rooms.

"I thought you liked your room," she said, surprised.

"I like it. I like it very much," I answered in haste. It was almost true. "But we'd have more fun if we slept in the same room."

My cousin looked at me with those caressing eyes of hers.

"Actually, I had thought about arranging the room in my style. You can't bring a bed of this size through the door. When we had the mattresses on the floor, we could hardly move. I think they built the beds at the same time as the house. Besides, I can't let you sleep on a mattress on the floor all summer."

I had to agree.

"We're not little girls anymore," she added, smiling. "We're too old to tell each other our secrets from bed to bed."

Sagrario and I had always shared our secrets at night. Even Nena talked to me until she fell asleep when we shared the room. I thought Irlanda would grow tired of me. She tried to teach me to play chess because I watched the others with admiration while they moved their pieces across the board, without hesitation, without doubting the move they had to make.

She made me sit at the table and taught me the names of the pieces and their movements. She started with a standard opening move, but I paid her little attention. I was enjoying taking the black king and queen and making them walk together over the squares.

"They're in love," I tired to explain. "They're taking a walk in the palace garden."

"It's a game of strategy, Natalia. It represents a battlefield and machinations of warfare."

"But a soldier can't kill a queen, it's not fair."

Irlanda looked exasperated.

"What's that got to do with chess? Look. This is how you move your piece. White wins. If you don't want to learn, just forget it."

I preferred not to say anything and go back to imagining the stories of the characters and why the bishops betrayed their old kings. Irlanda didn't try to give me another lesson, and I regretted not having paid more attention to her.

We were so different. However hard I tried to grow up, she was always ahead of me. I was afraid of making her angry because if I did, I was afraid her presence wouldn't keep the turtle out of my nightmares.

Her parents stopped by the house every four or five days and brought us our mail and often meals in large pots. My uncle got excited about our work and often said we deserved a reward.

"Few workers would have worked so hard and produced these results in such a short time."

"Then why don't you pay us?" said Roberto.

"Do you want to get paid when you're living and eating for free all summer? You want more?"

Roberto squinted, not at all satisfied.

"It's so easy to talk about the results when it's someone else's work. We've cleaned up the whole woods all the way to the main road," he mumbled.

"Shut up, Roberto. They let you use the car. What else do you want?" Irlanda said, always reasonable, always siding with the grown-ups.

"Satisfaction from your work should be enough reward. Aren't you ashamed, making a scene in front of your cousin?"

"I'm sure my cousin never talks back to her parents."

I looked up, surprised to find myself included in their conversation. My sisters and I lived wrapped up in the cocoon of our parents' protection, not knowing how much things cost or how much they should cost. Sitting on her bed, Nena and I combed Sagrario's hair and watched over her. Our parents smiled at us, but it was a tired smile when things were not going well, or a slightly wider smile when things were getting better. They kept track of the medicines and sent me to buy them when they ran out.

That was our job, and it had never occurred to me that anyone could change anything. Obeying was an easy thing and gave me almost limitless freedom.

"Learn from the girls, Roberto. Keep quiet, work hard, and don't complain."

That was true. We girls didn't complain, just as my uncle liked, maybe that's why we received some reward. One day my aunt showed us large chests scattered around the upper floor, five chests like large carved coffins, full of old clothes. One of them was in my room, and a part of the fabric of the wall was stuck on it. Irlanda was impressed with the carvings on the most beautiful chest.

"Look at this one. If it were sandpapered and varnished, wouldn't this look great in my room? It matches the color of my bed. It may have belonged to my room from the beginning."

Her mother raised her hand.

"This is not part of our inheritance, Irlanda. Those chests belonged to my sister and me. My mother left them to us. Grandmother kept keepsakes from her youth inside, but once she closed them, I don't think she had ever opened them, or at least she didn't for years. She didn't like old things, nor did she enjoy looking back on the past. My sister and I drew lots for the chests. Ours are the one in the hallway and the small pine chest. She left the others here, but I didn't buy them from her with the house. You'll have to ask Natalia before you do anything with them."

Irlanda made a grimace.

"We could divide them again."

"It wouldn't be fair," said my aunt.

"We could pay them."

"If they are willing to sell."

"But I was Grandmother's favorite."

I hurried to assure her that if Irlanda wanted the chest, she could have it.

"Don't encourage her, Natalia. Irlanda has to learn she can't always get her own way, she can't always get what she wants."

Irlanda muttered under her breath.

"We'll see," she said.

My aunt ignored her.

"You can open them as long as you keep them clean and don't damage them. At any rate," she added, "I don't think you'll find anything valuable inside."

I didn't think about the chests again until a few days later, one lazy afternoon when we had nothing to do. Irlanda played with her cat, and I stuck pressed plants to my herbarium sheets. During the previous days I had tried to remove fibers from the blue flowering plants, but they had rotted when I soaked them in the stream, and I hadn't been able to separate them, so I had given up, even though I had already got a bucket of ashes to bleach them with. I added them to my herbarium on the verge of despair and kept using the blue detergent in the boxes.

Then Irlanda let go of the cat and got up, brushing a few cat hairs off her clothes.

"Those chests... Aren't you curious?" she asked.

"The chests? Not really," I said, my mind wandering. "What could be inside?"

"Old clothes and dust, of course. But the amethysts? And the emerald brooches Grandmother talked about? The pearl strings that shone centuries ago? What about them?"

"Irlanda, all those things must have been sold years ago," I said and then kept quiet, hesitating.

I imagined the jewels wrapped in dark velvet, throbbing silently among the clothes and waiting to be awakened and appear on Irlanda's neck and arms. Then I would reach out my hand to touch them and they would crumble into dust. They would flee to the other side, and Sagrario could be adorned with the phantom gems.

"But we could find a magic lamp with a genie inside and ask him for three wishes. Just like in stories," I said.

Irlanda made an exasperated face.

"I've never known anyone so obsessed with fairy tales. You can be so childish sometimes."

I fondly thought about the characters from fairy tales, trying to make up for my cousin's coldness. "Don't get angry," I thought. "She may not know you, or her father told her fairy tales in a hurry before putting her to bed and she only thought of you as boogiemen in the night." "She's my cousin," I said, "but she's not like me. Don't take her with you." I suddenly imagined the rest of the summer in the country house, with another ghost and without Irlanda's bright presence to keep the dark world away. Irlanda kept staring at me.

"Natalia, you have your head in the clouds. Why don't we try to open them?" she said. "I can't stop thinking about them."

"Now?"

"We're bored like old women mending socks."

I wasn't bored, but I put the plants away and followed her. We looked for the keys to the chests among the jumble of unfamiliar, rusty keys, which hung behind the door and swung in the wind. We tried one key after another, but the keys got bent when we turned them in the locks, and the right keys must have got lost years ago. Then we sat down on the floor, exhausted but laughing, with our backs against the chests and our hands coarse and rusty.

"Now we know why Grandmother never opened the chests."

Irlanda stretched like a cat, and we called Roberto and Gabriel. They carefully studied the locks and tried all the keys while Irlanda and I became impatient and exasperated. Roberto wrestled with the lock. He poked at it with the penknife I gave him, then searched a toolbox and took out another bundle of keys.

"Let's not waste any more time," said Irlanda. "Break them open. There's no point treating them carefully. No one is going to use them anyway."

For a moment, I thought those chests were mine, that I would want to use them someday. But I was curious about the magic lamp, so I said nothing. Besides, the curtains by the open window swayed inward, and I was afraid Sagrario would come out of her tree and her tortured head would appear, nosing around the windows and timbers of the dying and decaying house.

The boys inserted wedges, which left marks on the edge of the wood, and I feared my aunt's reaction. The lids of the chests gave way, and the boys carefully opened them. Both of them were agile and tall, and I thought they could tear me into pieces, that Roberto could turn and slap me at that moment, and that Gabriel could bash in my head with the mallet and nobody could stop him. I imagined myself frail and worn-out like Sagrario under the pillow and her hands made of white fibers clinging around my neck, pushing me toward the open road in my dreams. I saw the veins in her tense arms and almost forgot about the chests.

The first two were a disappointment. The clothes appeared moth-eaten, and we found a nest of rats with eyes still closed at the bottom of the second chest. The bluish cat perked up its ears. We had more luck with the next ones. The wood was hard and had iron fittings. The lid burst open, and the fabrics puffed up, as if they had been kept longer than they were supposed to and fluffed up with starch. They came back to life with their ghosts inside and the same air they had breathed years ago. The clothes remained intact, together with the smell of close air, mint leaves, and mothballs.

There we found Grandmother's scrapbook, so similar to the ones my mother still made, filled with notes from the memorable days, pressed flowers, and pieces of lace used as bookmarks. Irlanda laughed, as if she received a handful of candy. Her laughter lingered between the pages of the scrapbook, like the voices in the walls, the smiles in the pearls, and death floating through the night mist. The cat had eaten the rats, but we hadn't even noticed.

6

*I*rlanda and I had our first argument the next day in front of the party dresses from the fourth chest. When we found them, we both screamed and laughed in excitement. We searched through the jumble of colored fabrics and hung the dresses on the shutters, imagining ourselves fairy tale princesses.

The cord of the amethyst necklace was broken. Only two or three beads were left, scattered in the bottom of the chest. We plunged into it like pearl divers and counted them many times, but each time arrived at a different number. We flicked open the fans and furiously stirred the air with the peacock feathers. In each of them a blue eye stared back at us, and I looked away to avoid the unblinking eye. And there were bridal veils, dresses with the flimsy embroidery like a spider's web, a sword, and a dagger with turquoises encrusted in its rusty handle.

My aunt came to the house that day. She gave a weak smile

when she saw us happy. "They're beautiful, aren't they? I didn't think they would be so well preserved. They don't even smell of mothballs. Which chest did you find them in?"

Irlanda smoothed the skirt of one of the dresses. She seemed absorbed. "Does it matter? One of the chests was full of rats. We should divide them half and half."

"I told you to remember where they were. What were you thinking, Irlanda? What was in your chests is yours and the rest belongs to Natalia. I hope you didn't do the same with the rest of the house. I expect that you divided what you found in the closets and in the house between the two of you."

My cousin opened her mouth, surprised. "But this house is mine."

"You had agreed to share everything with your cousin if she came to help you." My aunt turned toward me. "Didn't she give you anything?"

I had to shake my head. My aunt twisted her mouth.

"Irlanda, I'm very upset with you. Greed is one of the most contemptible vices. Your father and I didn't teach you to be like that. If that's what they teach you in your school, we'll have to think about finding you a less exclusive and more humane one."

Irlanda jerked up her head, but said nothing. My aunt kept talking.

"I want you to apologize to your cousin and make good the damage right now."

She came closer and mumbled an apology. I assured her that she had nothing to apologize for.

"I wouldn't think of taking anything that doesn't belong to me. And nothing in this house is mine. Please don't scold her. Irlanda is so sweet to me."

"I'm leaving," my aunt said. "I'm in a bad mood. You've ruined my day."

The two of us stopped talking, looking down at the floor, and went down to the kitchen to put away the food and prepare breakfast. I kept quiet, feeling vaguely ashamed that I didn't match up to my cousin's haughty bearing. Much later, when I thought she was taking her siesta, Irlanda called me. She had opened the fourth chest, caressed the yellowish tulles, and shook her head.

"We'll share them out, of course," she said. "You know how stubborn my mother can be once she gets something into her head."

I smiled.

"That's fine. Let's share them as you say."

Irlanda looked at me. I saw the flick of disappointment in her eyes. She kept talking.

"But, Natalia, think about it. What do you need them for? I would love to wear old dresses at a party. I'm cooped up here all summer, but we're going to have another party in the fall and a Christmas dance. Do you ever go to a party? Besides, those dresses are tight. Look at the waist. Do you think you'll use them? I can barely fit into them," she continued, placing one over her body. She did a few dance steps, then eyed me up and down as if measuring me. "Well, you'll know. You'll know what to do with them, whether you'd rather have them lost in oblivion like before. Maybe you want to keep them tucked away so that nobody will see them. You can always admire them as relics."

"They're just as much mine as yours," I said and picked up Grandmother's scrapbook, which had fallen on the floor. "Maybe someday I'll wear them. You know what your mother said. Actually, I should get two thirds of them because you have no sisters."

"Too bad Sagrario is dead. If she were alive, you could have three quarters with my mother's blessing."

I stepped back, astonished. Irlanda's voice had sounded vile. She stood in front of me, smiling and sweet, taking revenge in her way for having to share the contents of the chests. I turned back and left her trying on hats and veils. I went out into the garden and began to cry, seated on one of the stone benches.

She had it all. She was beautiful and elegant. She had money and friends, a young mother and even a brother. I had nothing, nothing besides a sister who refused to stay in the cemetery and my nightmares about animals chasing me, and now she wanted to take those chests away from me.

The storm clouds cleared away. I dried my eyes and held the scrapbook tight. My rage made me unfair. There was Nena with her strange questions. And Mama and Papa and the hand-me-down love from Sagrario and my herbarium. I had to leave my plants for a few days, but maybe the scrapbook would keep me busy. I had collected so many plants that all the sheets were used, and the rest were all over the place, both outside and inside the house.

"Can't you put your weeds somewhere else? Hang them or find some other place. Take them away from here. Take them away from there," Irlanda kept asking me. "I'm afraid I'll step on them and break them. Of course," she would add, to make me angry, "I don't think they're worth anything."

The flowers stayed in the tower, sheltered from dampness. Almost every day I went up to check them and watch the sky change color, always running away from the clouds.

"You spend too much time with your weeds," Irlanda would say. "I don't know anyone so interested in plants. Don't you have any other hobbies? Reading, for example? Or playing sports, or playing chess?"

I had worked on my herbarium ever since Sagrario had stopped walking. I would bring plants and she would look up information in books and dictionaries to fill out index cards. Later my sister lost her interest, but I kept working on the collection. There were only a few sheets left from that time. I had replaced them with more beautiful samples or better pressed ones.

I saw Irlanda leaning over a marquetry box. Then I glanced at the apple tree behind the gallery of the living room. Sagrario wasn't there. Maybe she got caught between the branches of bay trees in the woods.

I thought maybe I was turning into a strange creature, cowering over the flower press and roaming through the field like a lunatic. I had decided to forget the herbarium for a while and find another hobby. Sagrario's voice came down from the woods in a softly nostalgic tone. *Leaving the world without being able to dance, without feeling kisses other than the imagined ones, without knowing pleasure other than looking toward the hidden corners of the park on sleepy afternoons.*

Then the scrapbook appeared. If Irlanda was right, I had made many mistakes before I met her. Maybe the world went around in a different way than I imagined. Maybe there was a life free from the constant ticking of the clock and the nightly chases in the circle of the ghosts. In those salons, young girls danced with their rightful suitors and played with purring cats. Life didn't torment them, nor did death pursue them.

Only one life to live and this will be yours. With your memories, with the seconds flying by and timid lies to prolong it. And the clock doesn't stop and ends in your death…. How horrible, how horrible.

There was something more than the void of the world behind the corners we didn't turn. If I had been wrong, there wasn't much I could do. It was useless to cling to the memories of the past. Then I shook my head. "It's one thing to give up the herbarium," I thought, "but another to start building the world from scratch." I got up and left the garden to set off for the meadow.

The soil of the fields around the hill spread out before me, ploughed and bleeding, and feeding corn. Beyond the hill, a blue large-wheeled harvester piled up yellow grass, so quiet that it seemed very far away. At the edge of the road, a few drunken butterflies passed me and got lost among the wheat field splashed with poppies and cornflowers. I took a deep breath. "No more plants," I thought.

My anger against Irlanda was dying down. I knew those dresses were already hers. "I'm going to give them to her when I go back," I decided. "What do I need those old rags for? Now that Sagrario is gone, I have only Irlanda to guide me on the path to my new life. It's going to be a life so new and so happy that I won't even need clothes, or food, or none of what I needed before." I felt generous. The magpies croaked, agreeing with me.

The meadow stretched behind the tree-covered hill. It had been mine since I had found it. It was an enchanted place, and no dark shadows would come near because I had drawn a circle with an ash wand. Besides, I had a stream, and the ghosts can't cross running water.

There my sister and I had climbed the trees and begged the grown-ups to build us the small hut. Everything that wasn't from my world had to stay outside. Whenever the grown-ups came closer to watch over us, we would drop stones into the stream. Suddenly, they would complain about the cold, their necks buried between their shoulders, and leave us alone again. *Are you awake, Natalia? You must be asleep. I don't hear your voice, so you must be asleep.* Under the shadow of the trees, on the north corner, there were still pale jonquils and yellow daffodils.

Then I was startled. At the spring bend, near the road, I saw Gabriel in front of the trunk of an old chestnut tree. He stood with his back toward me. Then he turned and called me.

"It's drying," he said, pointing to the tree. "There are only few of them left. Now they plant trees for timber only." He paused and continued without looking at me, playing with a large medallion hanging from his neck. "What is it? A chestnut tree?"

"Yes," I said, lowering my eyes. Because I didn't want to upset Irlanda and her girlfriends again, I avoided talking to him. He moved as if floating in the air, and his eyes had the ghostly stare of those who have taken part in dark dances.

"In this area they say that for each dead chestnut tree a man has died."

"Not exactly," I corrected him. "The souls of the dead are hiding in chestnut trees. Also in oaks, service trees, and elders. Elder trees are witches, so you have to ask them for permission before you cut them. Otherwise they bleed and put a curse on you."

"What curse?"

"I don't know. Just a curse."

I knew perfectly well what curse it was, but it wouldn't be wise to reveal it to that creature, who tried hard to stay in this reality. It was best not to say anything and not to talk about these subjects. Otherwise, the army of lonely ghosts would come to his door and force him to join the dance of the curse. I imagined him tracing the footprints of visitors from the other side on the dewy grass during one of his morning strolls. Gabriel plunged his fingers into the moss on the bark.

"I learned the saying in a different way. When my father died, one of my grandmother's friends said it was a punishment for having cut down the chestnut tree in the backyard. It was half rotten and blocked all the light from the kitchen window. But the thing is, my father had it cut down. He killed himself a week later."

I said nothing.

"Another one," he repeated. "Another dry chestnut. Are you going for a walk? Are you going back to eat?"

"Yes…"

"Don't go very far. The other day they killed a snake at the bend in the road toward the village."

I felt uncomfortable and began to walk toward the meadow without saying goodbye. His long hair and his hands too delicate to work in the fields, Gabriel was slippery like a silk handkerchief. That was no doubt what they had found at the bend—a twisted, rustling handkerchief, not a triangular-headed snake.

I remembered his eyes, but the pupils, though they darkened, still kept their usual shapes, so the snake ghost hadn't possessed him. Not yet. "I'll have to warn him not to walk alone under the trees or they'll take him away," I thought. He headed toward the house. Looking down from the hilltop, I saw him join Roberto and go into the house.

In the meantime, I reached the meadow. The iron gate was closed. I jumped over the stream three times and made sure the magic circle hadn't been broken. Things went on almost as usual, almost as if I kept revisiting them in my memory. *Are you sleeping, Natalia? You sound so far away, you must be sleeping. Are you dreaming? Tell me your dreams. I've been sleeping for such a long time that I don't have time for dreams anymore. Another chestnut tree. Another chestnut tree. Don't go away. I've been sleeping a long time.*

When I felt safe, I looked for the site of the small hut and grabbed several jonquils, but the calmness had vanished despite my precautions. I noticed something strange in the meadow. Gabriel's voice followed me, and the smug curve of his lips came together with the image of the snake crawling among the tight dresses.

That idea left me with more questions than answers. Irlanda's waist was so small, you could wrap one hand around it. I measured my waist with my hands, feeling restless. I'd seen Sagrario grow thin in bed, forcing herself to eat, and fading into nothing. Every day, after dinner, I would sit to eat again, until my eyes filled with tears, trying to be strong, sturdy, healthy. I consoled myself looking at my reflection in the mirror and seeing death defeated. And now I was defeated by the narrow dresses.

I decided death would be satisfied with Sagrario, that I wouldn't be in danger, even if I stopped eating. Anyway, I began to want those dresses. I leaned over the stream, but the water ran too fast to reflect my image.

The grown-ups sometimes told they had found trout in the stream, but they had to be made-up stories. There had been no fish there. Maybe a river spirit combing her hair, or a fish-toothed newt sticking its head out of the water. Even so, they would hardly come to tempt someone because the river spirits were mute and shy. They would only steal my face in the water, but I was safe, because they always preferred fair-haired people.

Anyway, I still remembered my face without looking in a mirror. For a moment, I imagined myself dressed in a sheer dress and an impossible corset and getting out of a carriage. Irlanda's two friends held the train of my tulle dress splashed with diamonds and tried to flatter me without drawing anyone's attention. The garden fountain gurgled with water of violets. The palace covered with silver flakes shone under the moon. There the prince waited for me.

Like an old memory, the idea of sitting on a bench with a book in my lap came to me—I would sit while I waited until someone sat next to me, but I felt exasperated because I couldn't see the face of Sagrario's love. The only thing I remembered was the way he smoothed the creases in his pants. I sat down to remember more. The stars and mist surrounding love in the poems appeared only when I imagined the palace garden, with a prince, but like in my dreams, I could only see his eyes. Definitely, the time was passing, and I was going away from my riverbed, from my sister. The time was coming when I'd have to grow up.

I wandered around the meadow for a long time. On the way home, worried about the strange presence of something that didn't belong to me in my world, I plucked a leaf from the chestnut tree and with one finger traced its veins, trying to find secret messages.

7

*I*rlanda obeyed her mother. When I went back to the house, she had already divided the dresses. She was even considerate enough to give me two of the most beautiful ones, which was a graceful gesture. She had kept two bridal veils and all the white dresses for herself. I couldn't enjoy my victory. The quarrel in the afternoon still stung me. I felt that it was nothing more than a concession on her part.

I looked on the bright side. Irlanda's cutting remarks didn't bother me. Then I cared about only a few things. I wanted to make a successful transition to the world of grown-ups. I thought about going up to the elder tree to ask its old spirit if I could cut a branch and place it under my pillow for protection.

"If you keep walking by yourself there, ferns will grow on your clothes," said Roberto.

"Leave her alone," Irlanda told him. "You too go to the woods, but we don't tell you you'll come back with burrs on your back."

A letter from my mother was waiting for me on the table. I ran to the garden, tearing the envelope open. I read it while seated by the well parapet, under my window, protected by the black mass of bay trees with their stifling smell. The aromas wafted through the hot air as slowly as clouds carried by the wind. From one moment to the next, they enveloped me and faded. My mother talked about how things were slow and how the summer had filled the streets with invisible crickets. Nena sent me a beautiful drawing of a princess hidden away in a tower and a monstrous moon. I smiled as I spread the drawing. As I kept reading the letter, my mood changed.

Misfortunes have befallen us for a long time, but it's time to get up and get going. This year will be hard for you. Maybe you don't even want to think about it. But I think you should get ready to attend Irlanda's school. Your aunt and I have talked about it and we think it'll be best. You'll have more opportunities at your new school. Their foreign language program is very good, and there's an exchange program. Wouldn't you like to study in America for half a year? Besides Irlanda, you already have some friends at the school. I still don't know how my worries kept me from seeing things clearly before. I know I gave all my attention to your sister. Even though we wanted, we could never have afforded a school like that. You've been always an angel to me and Nena. Believe me, it distressed me to see what you had to give up, because I know we sacrificed you for your sister. But what would you have done, if you had been in my shoes? Someday you'll know what it feels like to be a parent.

Now, however much it hurts us, it's over. I want to make up to you and spoil you while I still can. Some day you'll leave my side and have a family of your own. I'll see you less often then. How fast you have grown! I try to fool myself sometimes into thinking that you're still a little girl. It's hard for me to accept that Nena is the only little girl I have left. She was really excited about your letter. Now she thinks of nothing but writing you.

Be a good girl, do as they say, and learn from Irlanda. I'm very glad you can change schools. Nothing was hurting me more than to see my niece turn into a young lady while my girls were forced to grow up too soon, bearing burdens that no one should be asked to bear. Call us when you can. Your father sends a kiss, Nena a drawing, and I all my love.

My mother, so kind and reserved. The world no longer belonged to people like her. She should have been born in her grandmother's time, when ladies played the piano and composed short letters, and handed out bread to the poor. Her white hands, her sad, noble bearing didn't suit the world where things changed so fast. Just as you learned one thing, it was already getting old, like the soft fabrics in the chests.

It was getting late. The evening sky wasn't nearly as red as it had been the week before. The clouds were becoming tinged with violet. I breathed in the smell of the bay trees. I supposed no spirit could live forever in those fragrant branches without going crazy. So I thought I would be safe there, even though it was getting dark.

I tried to decide whether going to Irlanda's school was good news or bad. I wasn't crazy about those girls. The girls at my school also worried about silly things and didn't know how to deal with serious life issues. Then I remembered I had chosen the dances and princess dresses in the meadow. I could easily imagine them in that atmosphere, with the boy with a white rose whose name I forgot.

Then I saw Gabriel walking toward me, and I froze. I wanted to hide the letter or at least act naturally. For the second time that day he came near me. "He could be one of the ghosts," I said to myself. "He has turned into Gabriel because he can't stand the smell of bay trees." He sat on the other side of the well, in front of me. I looked at him out of the corner of my eye. The metal filigree framed his body.

"Aren't you hungry? We've started dinner, and almost everything is gone."

I shook my head. He leaned over the well toward me, and I cowered back. I remembered his strength and how his arms became tense when he grasped the mallet. I was again afraid of dying. I promised myself I would eat well and go back to the meadow to cross the stream as many times as necessary. *Are you asleep? Don't you remember? Sleep tight.* He had only picked up the drawing from the letter and looked at it, smiling.

"My baby sister sent it to me," I said, relieved.

"Is this you?" he asked. He moved the drawing away from his face and compared it to me. "No, your hair is darker. It looks more like Irlanda."

"Nena is only five, but she's so quiet and formal that she seems like a grown-up."

"Children stop being children when they see disease and death. I didn't know you had another sister. They only told me about Sagrario."

I turned toward him. Since I had arrived, no one had mentioned my sisters, nor had they asked about them, except Irlanda's cutting comment that morning. Sagrario appeared again, half hidden behind the weeds and chestnut trees in the woods. Gabriel looked around, but he didn't seem to notice her. I was relieved to realize that despite the strange look in his eyes he wasn't looking out through windows from the dark world.

But I could easily imagine him wandering through the night with a frozen smile on the head he carried under his arm, leaving a trail of blood to alert someone to his death. "I found sad omens in my path, Mother. I still don't know whether I'm alive or dead," I hummed, remembering the song.

"When Sagrario died, I thought Nena wouldn't understand. At the funeral she played with the flowers sewed on the cloth covering the altar. My parents expected questions, they expected her to think Sagrario was asleep. But Nena understood everything. She perfectly remembers who attended the burial and who didn't, who left flowers and who didn't. Sometimes she draws how she saw Sagrario at the wake, lying still and thin. The first time she showed us one of those drawings, my mother burst into tears. I tried to convince her that it was a princess sleeping in a glass coffin."

"You must be heartbroken."

I remembered my mother's horrified face and nodded. Sagrario raised her arm and waved to me from a distance. Tears brimmed my eyes, and I brought a hand to my face. My chest hurt as if I had eaten something very bitter, or as if I were on the verge of tears, but I wasn't at all sure that it was because of my sister.

I turned around and stared down into the well, which smelled damp, like Sagrario's turtle's damp scaly body. Gabriel didn't try to console me. He listened as if he were hearing something distant, something that didn't concern him at all. With the same quietness, my mother had looked at the other mourners at the burial, in her black high-collared dress and the gold crucifix on her chest.

"I was about seven when the chestnut tree was cut down. I remember I used to play by the tree and its trunk was infested with white worms hiding in small holes. A while later, my father shot himself in the head. I was playing with my Meccano when I heard the shot. I thought it was a firecracker hidden in a hollow of the wall, and it had knocked out a brick. Firecrackers could do that, as I saw it the previous week. People ran around the house, left blood-soaked towels on the carpet, called for an ambulance, and cried, paying no attention to me. Somebody must have died, I thought. There were more people, more noises, more sirens of ambulances, more blood nobody bothered to hide, more screams. Nobody remembered to tell me it was my father who died. I clung to the staircase rungs, sat on the stairs, and went upstairs, one step at a time, to my room. I kept playing with my Meccano until somebody came for me."

His voice echoed back from the bottom of the well. That night the moon would rise over the water and varnish Gabriel's words. The next day I would find them climbing toward my window, silvery and transparent like soap bubbles. *Are you sleeping, Natalia? Are you sure you're awake?* Maybe his words would banish the goblins from my nightmares. But maybe they would let the turtle stay if it was already inside my room.

"That morning I'd asked him to wrestle with me. He promised me the red car I wanted for my birthday. He had lifted me up and hoisted me on his shoulders. I clung to his hair. I've often tried to imagine what was going on inside his head when he tried to destroy it that way. Sometimes I feel I can't control my own head, but I'm terrified of what I may find on the other side. What if there's nothing there? And suddenly, after learning how to think, we have to start all over in another world, be born again, grow up, discover that world, then kill ourselves because we can't stand it, and be born here again?"

I knew that was the way Sagrario liked it.

"I don't think there's any other world besides this," I said. "I think everything is here. Life begins and ends here, it repeats many times, and nothing is as complicated as it seems. I often have a feeling that I'm going through something I have already gone through and finding myself on paths I have walked before, like a story that keeps repeating itself."

"I wish I could think like that. Nothing after this world, one simple existence, and then rest."

I had said nothing about rest, but he had so completely misunderstood me that there was no point in explaining to him.

Despite everything, maybe he was a messenger from the dark side, and he was testing me. He seemed human, but the line of his lips was too cold, and a grim image of his figure reflected in the ironwork of the well.

"Death in childhood is sad," he said finally.

His shadow fell at my feet. He looked toward the grove. His neck was marked by the same mild tension Irlanda had in her limbs, like all slim persons. He looked at me again. He extended his arm and pointed to the path toward the house. The well was not a fountain smelling of violets, nor had the moon risen, but I had already dreamed of that.

I ate very little. Irlanda, maybe still worried about the quarrel of the morning, asked me if I was all right. I nodded and blamed the heat.

"We're being cooked over a slow fire. It's going to be even hotter tomorrow," said Roberto. "But Irlanda suggested we have dinner in the gallery living room. The breeze enters there. Maybe the heat will let up."

"We have the food my mother has just made," said Irlanda, excited. "I want to decorate the table like a formal party. The way they should have decorated it for the spring gala, which was so fussy and artificial. With many flowers and gold and all the windows shining and the floors polished."

I was pleased things had suddenly turned out the way I wanted, and dances would start soon. In the morning, when Roberto was outside checking traps and Irlanda still asleep, I traced a circle around the house with a wand of ash. So we could open the gallery windows without letting some shadow get in. I only left a small gap where I placed a bay branch so that Sagrario could perch on it and spy on us from outside the house, with her waxen face floating in the darkness.

The day passed quickly as there was a lot to do. We looked for candles and candelabra and cleaned the chandelier, which was too old to repair. Irlanda put one of the friar's chairs on the table and climbed on top of it to wipe the chandelier prisms with a cloth. She detached a chain of crystal teardrops and spread it over the table. Then we had to start all over again, because the cat clung to the teardrops, and we couldn't make him let go of them.

Roberto was trying to fix the cuckoo clock, which had been broken as far back as I could remember. He repaired the bellows and tried to move it with his finger. The cry of the cuckoo pursued us the whole afternoon, until at last the little windows opened on the hour and let the cuckoo pop out. Irlanda and I rushed to see the cuckoo.

"It's very charming," said Irlanda. "Too bad we don't have music!"

"You can sing something," said her brother. "If it's not too cold, we could go outside and take a walk in the middle of the night."

After dinner, we felt exhausted, but very proud of our work. On the door connected to the hallway, we had hung two pieces of old cloth embroidered with gold and green threads. We wanted to light the fireplace, but it was getting so hot that we made do with crumpled silver paper instead of real flames. The table was adorned with red apples, moss, and grayish eucalyptus leaves. The four high-backed chairs were arranged around the table. Irlanda and I set the table, with a surprise wrapped in each napkin—a figurine, a porcelain locket, a lace handkerchief.

Gabriel brought two silver ten-armed candelabra, except that one of them was missing an arm. He had found them in his room, but he didn't know how to clean them. When he handed them to me, he held my hand for a moment.

"I didn't give you back the drawing," he mumbled. He slipped the drawing of the princess in the tower into my robe pocket.

He moved away, and I could see the delicate tension in his

neck again. I followed him with my eyes for a moment. Then I was startled. Tilting her head, Irlanda was watching me with those elusive eyes behind lashes. I said nothing. I cleaned the candelabra and entwined a green creeper vine around them. The cuckoo clock announced nine thirty. Suddenly, it got dark.

Then we ran to get dressed, and I drew water from the well to wash my face and make my cheeks pink from the cold. In my luggage I kept Sagrario's green dress with an ivory lace collar and tassels. She had worn it at an award ceremony a year earlier, and it had the wide flare that covered her legs. The cloudy mirror cast back my image, green and trembling, as if I were leaning over a pool of water or a piece of metal. *Are you asleep?*

Irlanda appeared for dinner wearing a white dress from the chest. She looked like an antique doll in the middle of the newly decorated living room. I gaped when she came in. I gave her a resentful glance, which she spurned, proud. She smiled at Gabriel, and he, who was biting his green medallion, blinked, surprised. She sat at the head of the table. All eyes were on Irlanda that night.

She fluttered her hands while she ate. She was witty, smiling, as sweet to me as if she were my own sister. When we asked, she sang with an expressive voice. I had never heard her sing before. We opened a bottle of wine and drank a toast to her, but she modestly refused to sing again.

The cat purred at her feet, swishing his blue tail now and then. I felt distant, strange, guilty. The wine had made me feel like crying. "It's not Irlanda's fault," I told myself. That's how she was. Slender like a reed, charming, and perfect. She was my cousin and all I had. I repeated this over and over again, smiling like a robot, even though my smiles no longer attracted Gabriel's mysterious eyes.

The summer offered us the most beautiful stars, but they seemed to have veered crookedly and perversely from their paths, making my skin shiver after the persistent and oppressive heat. "Maybe it's just a dream." In the depth of night, the gallery windows cast Irlanda's glowing reflection and transformed it into a fairy floating in the darkness.

I peered into the shadows, expecting to find Sagrario. But my sister had left me to dance with the ghosts of her circle. She had left me Irlanda's reflection in her place. The workings of the clock on the wall had grown young, and the cuckoo stuck its head out to see us only twice. But that was the longest night of my life.

8

*I*rlanda had us twisted around her little finger. After that night, so sure of her power over us, she didn't seek my company as often as before. Even though our paths parted, I should probably have repaid her kindness and summer hospitality by trailing after her.

The image of those strange girlfriends, so submissive, made it impossible for me to do so. I preferred to feel abandoned and alone, two feelings already familiar to me, rather than be drawn into Irlanda's magnetic field, from which nobody seemed to know how to escape. I hoped one day to repeat that gesture of the sensible brunette, who lifted her shoulders with relief when she left us.

Alone by choice, I strayed from the path that led to the new world I still longed for in silence. I hardly worked. There was nothing left for me to do, as I wasn't interested in plants anymore. I shut myself up in my room, rested on my elbows on the windowsill facing the well, and sat on one of the chests of discord. I drifted away from reality. Small clouds flew across the sky, which became less red and more violet by the day.

Disheartened, I felt some signs of autumn approaching. My time of exile was coming to an end. I would be going home soon, and it would all turn out to be a bittersweet dream. I would spare only a moment, an hour, a few hours remembering that summer—and nothing more.

My cousins would appear in the distance, walking slowly. Occasionally Irlanda laughed, tossing back her head. I drew away from the window, consoled by the fact that Gabriel wasn't with them. Maybe he walked through the woods, looking for chestnut trees to save, and searching for a way to unlock my heart. We would live forever in the old country house with a wrought-iron fence that bordered the land keeping us safe from evil creatures. And we would be would be happy, so blissfully happy.

Sometimes, when my aunt paid a surprise visit, she would get mad at me because I wasn't going outside.

"What am I supposed to tell your mother if you go home pale and skinny? I want you to run and jump outside like a lizard. When you return from vacation, you should have put on some weight and look tanned and beautiful."

And then Irlanda, with a smile, invited me to join them. Her brother didn't argue with her anymore and looked at her with awe. He resembled their father as Irlanda did their mother. However, occasionally, they made the same gestures, even though Roberto lacked his sister's charm and the calculated grace of her movements. When he talked, he would let his words hang in the air for a moment, until Irlanda told him by word or gesture that she agreed with him. Then he would talk with the confidence he lacked before.

We had finished cleaning the house a few days earlier, and we waited for my aunt and uncle to return from their two-week vacation. Afternoons died quietly, turning purple, bringing us the time of harvest. The machines swallowed the grass and spewed up rolls of hay, which were later covered with black plastic. The grass slowly rotted and stunk, but the farm animals still ate it. The work was finished in a few days. I remembered the time when the farmers still used ox carts. The squeak of the axle was heard in the distance, as they brought the grass tied with ropes from the path toward the house. I looked at the red machines with a certain resentment for robbing me of the past.

One sunny Thursday, Roberto obliged me, with an imperial gesture so like one of his sister's that it was almost a parody, to leave my room and go with them to the meadow. Irlanda wanted to revisit the places they had known when they were little, and they didn't want to leave me alone in the house.

Gabriel and Irlanda were waiting for us in the garden. Irlanda had a parasol that looked adorable on her but would have looked grotesque on other girls. She also held two large roses, one purple and the other white, in her hands. She stuck one into my hair, and she held another between her fingers. Strangely, it stayed fresh for hours.

The meadow, their latest invasion, seemed magical and dark to them, a green box in the sun. They were surprised they hadn't discovered it before. The jonquils had withered. Now violets were in full bloom, hidden among the clover. Wild roses and an occasional shockingly blue gentian appeared among the blackberry vines.

"I've been here before," said Irlanda, forgetting for a moment that we took our walk to revisit the places we had been before. "When I was a little girl, my father fished trout in this stream. He built a playhouse out of the timbers that were left from the repair of the barn."

Irlanda sauntered toward the remains of the small hut. To my surprise, Gabriel followed her. They sat by themselves and forgot about us. I looked for an excuse to go back to the house, but Roberto kept me there, asking me the names of the plants around us. I spied on them, stealing sideways glances. Irlanda brought the white rose to her face and buried her nose in the petals. Gabriel gave a listless smile, almost reluctantly. The sun made a golden rim around his profile—his upright nose, his supernatural mouth, and his sweet jaw. The rest of his body remained in the shadow.

Men always fall in love with beautiful girls, but Gabriel had told me about his father's blood and about being born and dying countless times in different worlds. If he rubbed fern seed into his eyes, he would see my sister leaning against my shoulder, looking at me with curiosity as I answered my cousin's questions in my usual voice. I felt slightly safer than before.

Irlanda tried to fold her parasol. Gabriel took it from her and closed it so that she wouldn't hurt herself with its ribs. Then I didn't feel safe anymore, and I flung a red coat over my shoulders. I wished I were as strong as the boys so that I could smash my life to pieces and turn it into dust.

Finally, Roberto yawned with boredom, his eyes half closed. We headed back to the house. Irlanda threw her rose into the blackberry bushes, and I slipped it into my pocket. Gabriel wasn't being affectionate with her anymore. I went up the tower and pressed her rose, gnashing my teeth with rage. The magpies stirred on the wires.

During dinner, Roberto scribbled a list of provisions we had to buy in the village. We had run out of food. When my aunt and uncle were away, we would live on what we cooked and fruits from the orchard. He asked Irlanda to check the list, who added eggs and two chickens.

"Shall we go tomorrow then?" asked Irlanda.

"You know what's left in the kitchen better than I do. But you know what Mama said about sandwiches."

"We should stop feeding our cousin junk food," she said, in her voice of the first days, so pure and sweet. "Let's go tomorrow. We'll finish the week's work in two hours. If we slack off, we won't get anything done. And we're out of cat food."

"He'll be all right; he can eat our leftovers."

"That's what you think. Besides, we have to call Mama."

I smiled to myself, because that meant Gabriel and I would be alone the whole morning. Before going to bed, I rehearsed what I would say to him. I could make him a magic salad with nasturtium leaves and oil from the roses growing against the wall facing east, and we would have a picnic in the meadow. There we would talk about the other worlds where we would be born, where beautiful blonde girls didn't exist. Then the ox carts would appear again, turned into shiny carriages, and we would go back to the garden under the moonlight.

And we would live in the old country house. We would walk under the dark branches in the forest every night and ask the old spirits about our future. We would listen to hidden birds sing. One morning, he would surprise me with a vivid-colored bird in a golden cage. We would be so happy, so very happy. We would sit by the fire every night, until we were too old to talk and only the bird would sing.

I was suddenly terrified by the silence between us. I wanted to scream, wanted to call out Gabriel's name, but his hands, which hadn't wrinkled much with age, remained still on the armchair, only listening to the bird's song. He was so absorbed that he didn't notice how the silence and the distance curled the walls of the old house and our happiness, like a burning photograph. I drew breath. I would make a magic salad with nasturtium leaves, and we would eat it in the meadow. There we would talk, and there would be no silence between us.

But Irlanda went to bed late and woke with a headache. Roberto told me about it, worried, with the frustrated air of someone who can't bear suffering. He asked me to go to town with him. I had also inherited my mother's migraines. I felt sorry for Irlanda because it was a splendid day, and the pain doesn't go well together with beautiful mornings. I went upstairs and knocked on her door.

"Come in," she said.

It was the first time I entered Irlanda's private domain. I was dazzled by the light. The faded watery green walls kept the sunlight. At midday, the closet mirror would brim with light. Irlanda had a piece of white tulle over the bed as a mosquito net, a worm-eaten kneeling bench we had discarded, and hats adorned with fabric flowers and velvet ribbons instead of crucifixes.

"How's your headache?" I asked, almost whispering.

"I have a migraine," she said. "Sometimes in school it hurts so much, I think I'll faint."

In a glass cabinet, she kept the parasol with a mother-of-pearl handle, chocolate boxes, silver boxes, and all the small trinkets she sorted out during her siesta time. Her favorite chest served as a small table. A bouquet of white hawthorns and lilies dropped petals on the table once in a while.

"Do you need anything?" I asked.

"Close the shutters, please," she said. "Roberto left them open. He wants me to get up, but he doesn't understand I'd rather sleep this way, in semidarkness."

I sat beside her on the bed and took her hand. "Your brother wants to go to the village now. Do you want me to stay with you? Or do you want anything from the village?"

She shook her head. "No, thank you. I just want to be alone and quiet. I must have gotten too much sun yesterday."

"When I come back, I'll make you tea with mistletoe, sage, and linden leaves. It'll do you good."

"Don't forget food for my cat."

I left her in the dark room, carefully closing the door behind me. Roberto called me, and I ran for my shoes. My room was dark and damp. For a moment I rested my hand on the knob, distressed. I kicked off my shoes and opened the window wide, waving my arms so that the chemical smell of bug spray would go away with Sagrario's medicine, the guilty pillows. "This evening," I thought, "I'll take comfort from the sunset." Roberto honked the car horn, irritated, so I hurried down the stairs.

The village had a sad air of rainy places in summer. There were no new houses on the only street, but Roberto assured me that they planned to build a whole neighborhood toward the church. His father had bought a doctor's old house some years ago.

"It's the next thing we're going to fix," said Roberto. "We'll sell it when the village grows."

He pointed to the beautiful house, wide and tall, white and cinnamon, with glazed tiles under the eaves and a dusty palm tree as tall as the house. A green flowerpot was abandoned on one of the windowsills. Voices had faded, as they had faded into our tapestried walls. The furniture stood like ghosts under the white covers.

Roberto calculated aloud the price it would bring in a few years. I imagined him doing the same in the country house, measuring the living room with strides and asking his father whether they should split the garden or sell it as one lot. We made a detour to the back of the bakery. When we were inside the store, I looked back. The deserted street was intermittently lit by the neon green cross of the drugstore. The flowerpot, in the distance, watched me sadly.

We bought flour, meat, milk, chocolate, three dozen eggs, two chickens, oil, and a tray of pies, which Irlanda loved. Maybe the village came back to life on Sundays, when people filed into church, but as the morning began to cloud over, we had to clear our throats, stride into the stores, and wait for the shopkeepers to come out. They were suspicious of the modern peso, did sums by hand, and wrapped things in brown paper, meticulously folding the corners and holding them against their heart before handing them to us. The villagers had always hated us.

There was a time, the same era of the shiny amethysts, now dull, and the bridal veils interwoven with silver threads, when my family arrived in the country for the first time. They hired men of the village to build the walls of the summerhouse, which they built with rudimentary plumbing. They dragged stones from the mountains to raise the ogives of the chapel. My family's foremen visited the work site on horseback, looking only at the walls being slowly built, always too slow for their liking. They wheeled their horses around before the admiring eyes of the villagers.

But then the haughty members of the family arrived. The most arrogant among them was beautiful Hibernia, a cruel, intolerant woman, who wore stiff black riding dresses, patrolled her territory like a man, and wore sharp spurs on her leather boots. She laughed at her suitors and didn't marry anyone, which was an insult, as she was beautiful. She didn't hesitate to lash men and horses with her whip. The women in the family, covered with veils against the sun, whispered among themselves when they saw her come home at dusk, disheveled and tightlipped.

The summer passed, and the country house was left empty. The family went back to the city, fleeing from the boredom of endless rainy days. The lovers in the village had trysts in the gardens of the house. Never remaining still in their round nests, the pigeons flapped their wings as they flew over the roof.

One winter morning, Hibernia returned unexpectedly. A young man from the village, a chicken thief, had spent the night in a shed. He came out as soon as he saw her. Hibernia lashed him with her whip and slashed deep into his back and shoulders. Nobody ever knew what he did to deserve this punishment. Maybe she flew into a rage when she saw a stranger on her land.

She never revealed what happened. The village united against the family, and they withdrew into a hostile, unyielding silence.

The family married off Hibernia without her consent. Once, when she was a white-haired old woman with stony eyes, she returned to the house. She went from window to window, staring toward the distant hills.

We couldn't fight against the stories. We waited patiently as the shopkeepers laboriously wrapped the last of the bundles, handed them to us, and asked us to pay. I dialed my home number. I hung up after three rings. I dialed again. On the seventh ring, I hung up for the last time. It would have been unwise to try a third time, as I was so defenseless in the telephone booth in the middle of the street, with Roberto leaning against it, smoking and looking bored.

"Maybe they're out shopping with Nena."

We picked up the mail. I saw one letter from my mother and two for Irlanda. We set off on the return trip.

I kept watching Roberto's face, and he looked odder and odder. I just knew he was pretending to be calm. He smiled easily, but he preferred to make a scene rather than give in. He had the same face as someone who would sit on a park bench and become Sagrario's love, someone who could be also my love.

I imagined him being older, looking like his father, maybe with his father's mustache, speculating in land, sniffing out opportunities like a hyena and stirring up more resentment among the villagers. Then I regretted having judged him so harshly. He looked worried, and I remembered Irlanda and her migraine.

"Can you cook?" he asked suddenly.

"Not really," I said.

"Well, we're screwed," he mumbled, sounding more worried than before.

I looked down and didn't raise my eyes the rest of the way home.

It had cooled off. I rubbed my arms to warm myself. The air felt heavy as cold lead. Faraway, the eastern mountains were illuminated by lightning flashes that could be assailing the small mountain villages. The sheep in the open air bleated, curling up in blurred patches under the threat of rain.

The shutters of the house were open. I went up to Irlanda's room with two slices of cake. I called her name and waited. I opened the door carefully, but Irlanda wasn't there. I threw myself on the bed. Then I realized I hadn't seen Gabriel either. I ran downstairs so fast that I banged my side on the railing and tears came into my eyes. Men preferred pretty girls. And while I was in the village, Irlanda was feigning a headache. The light in her room, so bright... *Keep a close watch on them, because they'll steal your inheritance piece by piece, and you'll be left with nothing. And I'm not going to last very long.*

Suddenly this was the nightmare, and I was running, fleeing from something as dark as the turtle. I was in some indefinable place. I went around the house and found Roberto leaning against the wooden fence. He was talking to Gabriel.

"Natalia isn't going to like this," said Roberto.

"I forgot about that."

"I'm not going to like what?" I said, forcing a smile. My lips trembled, and I felt my heart beating in my throat.

"The men who work on your uncle's farm brought a cow. They expect it to give birth in a few days, but there's no room in their stables. They asked me if they could leave it here, and I said yes. I forgot about you."

I assured them it didn't bother me. "That's fine. But keep the cow out of my sight."

I saw myself milking a red horned monster, who pointed the turtle's sinister mouth at me. I shut my eyes tight, trying to focus on Gabriel, who was leaning against the wooden fence. With those boards, they had built us the small hut. I promised myself

I'd check them carefully, just to make sure that more of our boards with secrets scribbled on them had been used to mend the old fence.

I felt calm then. I asked them where Irlanda was. Gabriel pointed toward the meadow with a vague expression on his face. I began to run. I met her halfway down the path. Her migraine had disappeared, and she had rosy cheeks. I was happy to learn that she had spent the morning in the meadow, far from Gabriel. I took her hand, and we ran together toward the house, before the rain could soak us completely.

9

*T*hat night Irlanda appeared in my nightmares. I found myself in a pit. Even though I didn't see it, Sagrario's turtle was following me. I began to run with its invisible presence, but I knew
if I ran too fast, I would catch up with the turtle. If I stopped,
it would reach me. Irlanda peered into the pit. Then I realized
that I was inside the well of the garden. She sat on the parapet,
swinging her legs over my head. I shouted to keep her from falling. I forgot to run. Then it wasn't the turtle who caught me—it
was an angry cow, who gored me in the side.

I woke up with a real pain in my side, which I had hit when
I ran down the stairs to look for Irlanda. Trying to imitate the
bouquet in her room, I had picked a hawthorn flower and a lily
of the valley the day before. They smelled like mold in the well
in my dream. I opened the window and threw away the flowers.

I thought I would feel completely better soon, because I dared to get out of bed at night. It took some nerve to open the window in those days when the turtle was so active. Besides, Sagrario didn't visit me anymore. Far away among the hills, Hibernia's hellish horse galloped. Then I tucked myself into bed, waiting for daylight, which was slow to come into my room.

The previous afternoon had been cloudy, and it rained all day, from morning until night. At times, the rain seeped through the ceiling, and the sound of falling drops joined the ticking of the clock to measure time. I went into the gallery every few minutes, hoping the rain would stop, because I had nothing to do but sit by the fireplace and feed the fire with branches.

If Gabriel had been there, I could have asked him to teach me chess. He would be patient with me and let me win to make me think I was a quick learner. But I was alone. Sagrario no longer came to the windows as she used to do. Now I regretted not having given her a blanket to wrap around her against the cold night air. The ghostly bonfires wouldn't keep her warm.

Maybe Sagrario missed her bed, her warm blankets, or even her pillow. She was sensitive to cold. It was selfish of me not to think of her much lately. I broke the branches and cast them into the fire, hearing them crack on their path of death.

Irlanda was busy cutting pieces of paper and pasting them into her new books. I leafed through some of them when I got tired of watching the fire. But I felt her watchful eyes, as she was afraid I would drop her books, so I closed them on the table.

"Natalia, can't you keep still? Find something to do. You're making me nervous," she finally said.

"Where are the boys?"

"In the village."

In the village. Bored, I watched the rain fall. "It's raining as if it will never end."

"It's rainy this time of year. We were very lucky. The weather has been good this summer."

Why had they gone to the village? Maybe I would bundle up in my coat and boots and go for a short walk. I would call aloud to Sagrario through the fields. I would check the magic circle in the meadow so that nobody could get in. Maybe I would find Roberto's cigarette butts in the grass. Irlanda raised her head again.

"Why don't you go check if your plants are dry?"

"They are dry. I went up the tower this morning because I was afraid rain would ruin them."

"Then bake cookies. The stove is on. The boys loved your cookies the other day." I took a few steps toward the kitchen and heard Irlanda mutter. "Why can't you get interested in anything besides your stupid plants?"

I was looking for flour when the doorbell rang. It was one of the farmers, asking for the boys. The cow was calm, but he would check on it again in the afternoon. At any rate, Roberto knew where he lived. If we didn't mind, he intended to spend the night with the cow.

I told him we didn't mind, without consulting Irlanda first. Gabriel made decisions, so I didn't see why I too shouldn't make decisions.

The boys came back at midday. Only then did they tell us they had bought fireworks to throw another party before the grown-ups came back. We had been talking about this mythical party for days, as if when it was over we would have to face the unknown and unpleasant world. The boys carefully carried the wooden boxes so that the fireworks would stay dry. They told us not to go near the barn.

After lunch, the rain stopped for a while. The slate-colored clouds slowly turned brown along a slit the sun had opened. I leaned out of the kitchen window, longing for a rainbow in the gray sky. Then I grabbed Roberto's coat and rubber boots, and slipped through the back door, before it rained again and

Irlanda's sensible voice forced me to go back. I hid among the branches of bay trees. Then I ran toward the green meadow over the hill, softly calling my sister's name, suddenly afraid that she was no longer there, and that the machines would have devoured the violets and dried jonquils.

The stream meandered freely. The spell of the circle was broken, but that could be fixed. Irlanda's gestures remained, printed on the earth, fixed there by the rain-soaked grass for a long time, more intense around the hut, where the ground turned yellow from the sourness of her smiles, and almost imperceptible in the reeds in the corners.

I stood under the trees, which had turned gray like the sky. My mind drifted back to Irlanda. *Here they built me a playhouse. My brother and I would play for hours, fight over the key, and keep my father's fishing rod.* Irlanda's voice would rise each dusk, an alabaster image with the tiny parasol. *I've been here before.* That place wasn't mine. I closed the wire gate and wrapped the rope around it three times. I stood on tiptoe. For a while, I felt sorry to see the remains of the hut. I scratched the wooden board attached to the gate and broke into a run with my feet in the oversized boots.

I stopped to rest when I reached the hill. My lungs felt empty, and I gasped for breath. The old house bore the sun's pale stain in the corner where my room was, and it disappeared quickly, as the clear spot among the clouds was closing, threatening rain.

Near the dying chestnut tree, I heard steps and saw a shadow moving toward the spring. It was a strange boy, with his back toward me. He knelt down by the water and began to wash his shoulders, which were marked with red wounds.

He raised his head and seemed to look through me. I didn't hide. He didn't react either. No doubt he knew I wasn't his enemy. Trickles of blood flowed into the spring. He put his shirt back on and disappeared among the trees.

The clouds became heavy and a drizzle began to fall. Deep in thought, I walked toward the house. If the ghosts were so slow to die, I would never get the meadow back. Now it was invaded by the gurgling of water genies and falling rain. On rainy days like these, they would laugh, having reconquered their domain. I put the meadow out of my mind for good and walked slowly, putting one foot before the other and staggering as the boots made me lose my balance.

That night the calf was born. Everybody had stayed up till dawn, through an endless muggy night. The farmer called in the evening. The calf was coming out backward, and he asked the boys for help. At midnight Irlanda also wanted to go, and I was left alone.

I lay down on the couch in the living room, sick of the rain, the endless night, and empty hours. "It feels like November today," I decided, in a bad mood. "It's raining as if it were the end of the world. In days like these, I wish the world would end."

I was alone in the house for the first time. The wood in the windows creaked as if old Hibernia went on with her search, looking out the windows for the petty thief who had escaped from her. And the turtle came back.

I ran inside the ditch, as the turtle chased me. But this time, it was in front of me, opening and closing its mouth. I was paralyzed. The ditch went round and round, and no matter how much I ran, I couldn't find an end. I woke up, almost screaming. It took me a while to remember that I had killed that turtle a long time ago.

I groped for the glass of water on the night table and then remembered that I had made myself a bed on the couch in the living room. "You're awake now," I told myself. "You've come back. You're safe now." I felt my temples pounding, my mind racing back to the past. I was saved when I found myself by the fire, inside the circle I had drawn around the house. That turtle was dead.

When Sagrario was five or six years old, my parents bought her a large turtle. She couldn't get around too well, and the turtle was slow. I never liked to watch it crawl with its small feet. Nor did I enjoy watching it in the water, which showed its yellow belly. But Sagrario had grown fond of the creature. She even slept with the turtle, not afraid of crushing it.

One morning I woke, surprised by the damp smell. I opened my eyes and found the turtle's head an inch away, on my pillow, staring at me and opening and closing its black mouth. Squirming away from it, I was pinned against the wall. The turtle inched toward me on the sheets. Then it turned around, and kept crawling on the night table toward my sister's bed.

After that I was afraid I would find the turtle creeping over my body. I asked my parents to put it in a cage, but Sagrario enjoyed following it around the house. My mother didn't have the heart to take it away from her. She was very thin, and we already knew she wouldn't live very long.

I waited patiently for the creature to die the same way as the gold fish, but when I asked my father how old it was, he told me turtles could live for hundreds of years. I was frightened. I saw the turtle everywhere. Every time it looked bigger, more monstrous, and more disgusting.

I was in the kitchen, and the turtle was eating lettuce in its spot. My mother had gone out with my sister, and my father was asleep in his room. I grabbed the lettuce leaf, but the turtle didn't let go. I pulled the leaf, and the turtle, seizing it in its sharp jaws, dragged itself toward me. I hit it and stamped on it as if trying to free myself from a demon, until its neck went limp and it stopped moving. I touched its shell with the tip of my toe. It stayed still. Kicking it, I hid it under the kitchen table.

They found the turtle upside down in the evening. Everyone thought someone had crushed it with a chair. Sagrario cried for several days. She didn't want another turtle or another animal she could grow attached to and miss later. My sister looked out the window with a sad face. In the meantime, ever since the night the turtle died, it visited me. I woke up screaming. My mother comforted me, brought me a cup of hot milk with honey, and turned off the light again, but I couldn't go back to sleep.

The next day I buried my favorite doll and the most beautiful marble in my collection in a box, hoping to appease the turtle. I cried when I parted with my treasure, even though I knew I was doing the right thing. My sacrifice and remorse were useless. The dead monster rose from the dead to chase me night after night, as only ghosts and the dead did.

I heard the long and mournful lowing of the cow. I knew that night, just as the night the turtle died, I couldn't sleep anymore. I got up, washed my face, and remembered that I had started making cookies in the morning. I took the dough out again and began to knead it. Irlanda and the boys would have them for breakfast. I would put a kiss in one and keep it for Gabriel.

Later the cow's owner appeared. He drew two buckets of water, and invited me to see the calf.

"Animals aren't supposed to be born on a cement floor. Every farm should have a stable with weeds and grass, and things will be all right."

I leaned against the kitchen wall, feeling the hot air rush against the bruise on my side. The turtle had sniffed out a new life and come to snuff it out. I was the one who had held on to the calf in the cobweb of my dream, while my insensible sister was dancing God knew where. The calf owed its life to me. For the first time in my life I gave life to someone, instead of causing someone around me to disappear. Then I decided. I took the cookies out of the oven, wrapped them in a napkin, and went to the stables. Before I arrived, I heard laughter.

"I brought cookies," I said, as I entered. I peeked carefully into the stable, frightened by the smell of ammonia and blood.

The cow was tied in one corner, so I decided to take a step further. My cousins had separated the calf from its mother and were washing it. Their laughter grew louder when they saw me.

"I brought cookies," I repeated.

"Do you expect us to eat them here?" Roberto said, choking with laughter.

I asked what the matter was. A dark tide was rising inside me. I tried to smile, but I couldn't, because I hadn't stayed up all night with the others and shared their joy. It was too late to join them. Irlanda burst out laughing again.

"We have already named the calf."

And it was then, when they said that to me. I can swear it was then, because I still see the stall and the wet rag they had thrown down on the floor, and I smell the life of the stable—it was then that I began to hate Irlanda and the fate that cruelly refused to let me take part in the rituals of life.

I went back into the house, twisting the napkin in my hands, as the cookies crumbled to pieces. I found the books Irlanda was mending with paper on the living-room table. Next to them there was a plate with ripe plums and early grapes, with a blush layer of black fruits nobody had touched. I grabbed a handful of grapes, opened the books, and squeezed the grapes until only the skin was left in my hand. A pool of juice drenched and wrinkled the pages.

"This could be blood," I thought. "This could be blood. This could be blood." I spilled Irlanda's blood on her immaculate books. Then I kept imagining the whole house flooding with blood, her white dresses, her spotless room soaked in blood. "I wish it were her blood, Roberto's, Gabriel's and everyone else's. I wish to live alone in this house with Nena, my mother, and my sister Sagrario. I wish the cat would die—and my hypocrite aunt, my loan shark uncle, the villagers, the sewing nun, the caretaker, and her daughter, and everyone except us."

I went to bed, muttering awful things and hoping to find some evil spirit of death awake, a horse-sized, black dog with blazing eyes, with the skin of worms. I wanted it to find them in the stables, outside the magic circle, and devour them, leaving only the bones.

The avenging dog didn't come. When they went to bed, it was already day. They wouldn't appear again until the next evening. By then I would be calm and starving, nibbling the crumbled cookies in the napkin.

Nothing changed my habits, and there was no change in Irlanda. We would go for a walk together in the afternoons, as usual. The boys didn't seem to notice anything, but Irlanda barely looked at me when we planned our magnificent party. I went to bed every night, mouth tired from too much smiling. And I was thinking. The window over the well didn't just see me lost in the clouds and the tangled garden. I was deep in thought. If nothing helped me, if the spirits refused to come to my aid and the spells of the circles lost their power in a few hours, I had no choice but to give them up.

Roberto thought it funny to name the calf after me. He joked about it for days. Irlanda noticed my discomfort. Maybe sensing my distress, she reproached her brother tenderly, shining like the sun.

I stole sideways glances at Gabriel when he wasn't looking. He smiled as if nobody else existed in the world. The silence that circled us in my gloomy thoughts still held him. I think he didn't really see me. He was lost behind the walls of his secret room, to which only Irlanda's radiant smile had access back then.

10

*I*rlanda took charge of organizing the party. At first I thought I was lucky, because I had time to loaf around as I pleased and think about how complicated my world was becoming, but later I decided it was unfortunate, because she refused my offers to help with any of her work. Feeling resentful, I was surprised thinking that only she would take the credit.

For a couple days I kept insisting that she should let me help her. But Roberto didn't trust me. He had grown tired of my cookies. He was glad that his sister was in charge of everything, at least in the kitchen. Anyway, I had to admit that those two would be too much for me, and I was satisfied with what they had assigned me.

Irlanda had given us two orders: not to go near the kitchen or the gallery living room and look for beautiful clothes in the chests. She even gave us a free hand to pry into her prized belongings.

I took the boys to adjust their suits. We had three old uniforms, a little stained. I intended to make up for the rough time at the last dinner with a wonderful dress with velvet surplice that I had sewn undoing two old dresses. Roberto and Gabriel followed me everywhere, not knowing how to behave, not even how to move in their uniforms.

Feeling a bit embarrassed, I let the boys come into my room. I picked my pajamas up off the bed, rolled them into a ball, and hid them under the pillow. The cloudy mirror reflected only stains, but it was the only full-length mirror I could find. I knelt down beside my cousin with pins between my lips.

"Where did you learn to do that?" asked Roberto.

"In class," I mumbled.

"In what class? I had no idea they still taught sewing in school. What else do they teach you? Dressmaking and embroidery?"

"A woman should know how to sew," I answered shyly, even though I hated buttonholes and festoons. I tore one of the seams and undid the hem. I wished the sewing nun with a scared swallow's eyebrows could see me now. Then I remembered that I had sicked a ghost dog on her, and I felt better.

The army jackets didn't close and the pants were too short, so I spat out the pins. I thought about ironing the hems. Roberto turned to look around.

"This is a miserable room. Why don't you move to the red room? It's next to mine, and it's full of light all day long."

I shook my head. "The sun goes down behind the woods in a few hours. I can see the first stars. I like this better than light."

"It's very damp. It's cold."

We plugged in an old, small iron with an odd-shaped spout. I smoothed out the wrinkles of the pants to make them longer. The boys watched me with great interest, their arms crossed and keeping their distance from the table, as if the iron were a dangerous object. Gabriel was biting his green medallion. Irlanda called to me from downstairs.

"Natalia! What are you doing?"

"I'm ironing."

"Go down to the garden and pick some long-stemmed flowers for the table. I'm busy."

"So am I," I thought, but I obeyed without protest, because I wasn't alone. I was also worried about what the boys thought of me after I failed as a seamstress. I told them not to touch anything, because the iron could scorch if they weren't careful, even though they didn't seem eager to iron. I went out into the garden, and my ankles got wet. The weather had turned cold in the last few days. I wandered around aimlessly. We had finished putting almost all the flowers into the vases to brighten up the house during the gray afternoons. I could find only a bunch of red poppies, which amounted to nothing.

I thought about foxgloves laden with red bellflowers and woody nightshades growing by the rubble of the stables. I thought it fitting to decorate Irlanda's party only with poisonous plants. While she was unsuspecting, I could smear her cake with red berries and woody nightshade.

Nena would have loved it. I remembered I hadn't written to her for a while. I decided to bake a cake with foxglove flowers for her birthday, as a secret between us.

The farmer, who often came to the house after we allowed him to leave his cow there, closed the stable door. He gestured for me to approach. He carefully moved a few branches and put his hand on my shoulder, beckoning to me to look where he pointed.

"A cuckoo. You've never seen a cuckoo?"

In the bay branches, there was a nest with three little birds, three magpie chicks.

"The largest one is the cuckoo. The mother puts her egg into the magpie's nest, because cuckoos eat poisonous caterpillars, which would kill the chicks. See how smart they are. They choose a smaller bird to raise their chicks. When the cuckoo grows up, it stays as the owner of the nest."

He was middle aged, hardly any wrinkles in his face. His voice showed his admiration for the slyness of the cuckoo.

"What happens to the baby magpies?"

"The cuckoo throws them out of the nest."

The man began to walk away. I stayed watching the nest. "Take them," I thought. "Take them home and raise them before the cuckoo kills them." I knew if I moved the nest, the mother wouldn't come near it and the babies would starve to death. But I found it disgusting to reach out my hand and touch the baby birds. They had large hearts, beaks, and new feathers. "I'll come here every day and take care of the magpies," I decided, finally, because Irlanda was getting impatient. Maybe it wasn't a good idea to interfere with nature's law.

I struggled with the old iron and the uniforms during the whole afternoon, until I became bored. At the end, the increase was barely noticeable, but I was almost bursting with pride. Gabriel attached an empty sheath to his belt. It was supposed to hold a sword lost among the secrets of the chests. Roberto got dressed, seemingly forgetting something. When he had finished, he remembered.

"The fireworks," he said suddenly. "I haven't even prepared them."

"We could see them from the tower."

"No," said Roberto. "What are you thinking? That would be crazy. The tower is old. Something could fall on you."

"I go up almost every day to leave my plants, but nothing has happened to me."

"Well, you should stop doing that. The tower and the chapel are completely in ruins. And now with the fireworks. What if they catch fire and cause an accident? What would I say to my parents?"

"But I never carry matches or fire. I don't smoke. How would I cause an accident?"

Irlanda had the lost sword. She had cleaned it. Gabriel brandished it like a bold soldier, and let Irlanda adjust it. With a lace and ivory fan, an embroidered shawl around her shoulders, and satin shoes almost entirely hidden beneath the hem of her skirt, she had never been so beautiful before.

"Look what I've found," she said, showing us one of her Bibles with lists of names with dates following them on the first pages. The last rows were written in the same slanting, complex hand in the album. "It starts with my name and ends with mine," she continued, laughing.

The last name on the page was hers, with her date of birth neatly written. Irlanda was only three months older than me. Maybe Grandmother forgot Sagrairo and me, or lost the Bible. I hoped with all my heart that remorse for having left us out tormented her at the hour of her death.

"It doesn't start with your name," I said. "It says Hibernia here."

"Hibernia means Irlanda in Latin, Natalia. It means 'land of eternal ice.' My name has been around for at least a couple of centuries," she finished, with her laughter like a waterfall destroying my nerves.

At any rate, Hibernia the cruel was her name, with her Amazon riding outfits and a feather in her hat, whipping her horses with the same hands as Irlanda and exciting the same kind of admiration. I was amazed that I hadn't thought of it before, and that I had dreamed I was the one like her, with her gaze lost on the mountains in the horizon. I tried to remember what my name meant, whispering it many times, but only the image of the calf in the stable came into my mind.

Roberto got up, leaving the neatly folded napkin on the table.

"I'll look for a place to put the fireworks."

"Where?" asked Gabriel.

Roberto shrugged. "I don't know. It's hard to say. The tower was the best idea."

"Yes!" Irlanda exclaimed. "Roberto, from the tower. Imagine the view, under the starry sky, watching the fireworks from the tower. You can light them from the river. The tower, Roberto. I want the tower."

"But you've told me…" I began.

Roberto hesitated, not listening to me. "You'll have to be careful," he said. "We have secured the tower, but be careful. Stay only on the braced areas."

I lowered my head over my plate. I felt tears coming. Maybe Irlanda's voice changed my ideas and put them into new boxes, as I did with my gifts. Or maybe she had a talent for avoiding ridiculous scenes and her brother's scolding.

I swallowed the bitter knot in my throat, but it didn't help me. I was trying to frighten away death by not eating, so I was hungry. I made drawings with the fork on the crumbled cake and pushed it away. Then I sighed and calmed myself. Things couldn't possibly get any worse. Unless the dress came apart, things couldn't be worse.

That night we watched the fireworks from the old tower. Gabriel and Irlanda carefully leaned against the new handrail. Obedient, I stayed with my back against the wall, without watching the fireworks. I wanted to bury my head in the dry grass. I wanted to be covered with piles of dry red dust, feeling ants in my mouth and worms over my eyes, or having to face fire-spewing goblins with tentacle hands.

The old dress was tight around my waist and didn't let me lift my shoulders. "It's just a dream. I'm sleeping," I thought. I would wake up and have to kill the turtle and see Nena being born and read to Sagrario during desperate nights. But a voice looking for evil fingers inside me was laughing. *You aren't sleeping,*

Natalia. You never sleep. Are you too tired to tell ghosts from humans?

The fireworks continued for ten minutes. I bit my hand to keep from crying. Irlanda and Gabriel kissed each other as the fireworks exploded, and the smell of gunpowder filled the air. Irlanda looked at me out of the corner of her eye, certain that I wouldn't dare look back at her.

My name meant birth. I remembered it much later, when I was alone in my room, listening to the floor creak, as I didn't want to go out for several days. I was lying in bed, looking for familiar figures among damp patches on the ceiling. I was waiting for death to come, as I looked so much like one of the ghosts stalking in the shadows of the black bay trees. It was said that they rested in cold dark places during the day. Only after sunset did they come out, alone, thirsty for blood and life.

On the fifth morning of my confinement, Gabriel came to my room after Roberto had walked away, grumbling about me. I had refused to talk to him, as I was still upset about the incident at the tower. I was lying on the bed, dressed but completely disheveled. I felt so far away from everything, as if I were a cloud. Gabriel opened the door. His figure bounced off the mirror, reflected briefly on all the walls before being devoured.

While he talked, I couldn't keep my eyes off his mouth. One day he had leaned over the well toward me, holding out his hand. That afternoon by the well, when Sagrario's ghost appeared among the faraway trees, was such a long time ago that I'd forgotten about it, as my mind was occupied with so many other distressing afternoons that followed.

"Roberto is afraid to come near you," he said, sounding cheerful, "because of the way you treated him the last time. Where does it hurt? Do you have a fever?"

It's not too late, Gabriel, I thought. *You have nothing to tie you to her except for a few kisses in the tower.* His fairy-tale prince's profile, his sad, faraway gaze, got lost on the shutters hiding the grim afternoons. A red scratch mark ran across his arm and down his shoulder, hidden under his shirt. *Time will fly, and I'll turn into a water ghost, withered and evil by the well, covered with waterweed and sargasso. I'll call you to trap you in my deep, stagnant waters. But you can set me free. I was the princess in the tower, not Irlanda. You have your sword to open up the path.* Gabriel looked at me with pity.

"You must be getting homesick, but you'll be going home soon. We have only a few days left. Come with us. Let's have some fun. How can you stay in this room for hours, letting time slip away? Don't you get bored? Doesn't the dampness bother you?"

Run away with me. I'll find a way to sit by the fire and look at you. I won't let the silence linger over the fireplace. Make me believe it's not a dream. Gabriel didn't pay attention to me. He avoided looking at himself in the mirror and opened the window. Then he stepped toward the wall and peeled off some fabric. He kept throwing it away.

"My God," he murmured. "No wonder you're sick."

Under the tapestried walls, a layer of mold and cobwebs had grown. I dropped my head on the pillow.

"Get up right now," he ordered. "Take a shower and go out in the sun. And eat something. I picked red apples from the large tree. I know you like them. I'll move your things."

I wished life would go on like that, listening to his words, feeling that doing as he told me was enough to be safe, and imaging his body in the dark. He pulled me up off the bed and put a jacket on my shoulders. Just as he did that afternoon by the well, he offered his hand to lead me to the door. I wanted to kiss his hand.

The kitchen was deserted. I caressed the apples and bit one without much interest, thinking about the silent plague spreading through my dark room. Things were strange. They played hide-and-seek, nothing was what it appeared to be. The world kept going around and disrupting everything we knew.

Irlanda's cat lay beneath the midday sun. I crouched down to stroke his head. I remembered the time when I had been terrified of him and smiled. I felt grown up, almost like an old lady. Then the cat was startled, hurled himself against me, and scratched my face. I screamed. Roberto came running.

"What happened? What did you do to the cat?"

"I was just stroking him."

Roberto threw up his hands. "What made you want to play with him? You don't like animals."

Irlanda had taken the cat into her arms and buried her face in his bluish fur. "Poor baby. Are you scared?"

My cheek throbbed. I noticed I was bleeding. Roberto reacted finally and looked at my wound. "It's nothing. Just a scratch."

"He could have poked my eye out."

"You shouldn't have scared the cat. He wouldn't have done anything to you if you hadn't bothered him."

I pushed him away and put my hand over the wound. Roberto stepped back.

"You're crazy," he said. "Nobody understands you."

Gabriel came toward us. "Your things are in the red room." He looked at me and pointed at my cheek. "What's happened to you?"

"The cat has scratched her," Irlanda said with a shy smile.

I shoved Gabriel out of my way and ran from the kitchen.

"I don't want anyone to touch my things! I don't want to change rooms!" I shouted. "Stay away from me! Leave me alone!"

"You're crazy!" yelled Roberto. "Completely nuts!"

I shut the door behind me and rested against it, covering my ears with my hands and wishing them dead. Someday they would die, but I decided they should die right then and there. I asked Sagrario for help. I told time to hurry and bring death to them right away. "They're dead," I told the mirror. "Time has gone crazy and brought an end to them." But time kept ticking, and it only brought a few knocks on the door and Roberto's quiet voice.

"Natalia, be reasonable. Open the door. This room is bad for your health. It's covered with fungus, and you could get sick. Listen. Are you listening to me?" He paused for a moment. "I don't want you to make a scene. I thought you were a sensible girl. Do you hear me?"

"I don't want to!" I shouted. "I like the view toward the west, the garden with the well under the window, and this closet with a mirror swallowing everything it reflects. Why don't you leave me alone?"

"At least tonight," he said, after a pause. "If you insist on sleeping in this room, we'll remove the fabric tomorrow. I can have the wall plastered. But sleep in the red room tonight. Come out of there."

I kept quiet for a while. Sagrario and I used to sleep there. Maybe it was as good a place as any to find her that bitter night. I obeyed and followed them downstairs. I kept looking down at my plate. I didn't want to see their faces. I focused on my food and forced myself to swallow it, imagining each bite was a fulfilled desire. Nobody talked much. Roberto dominated the conversation, apparently pleased with the sound of his own voice.

The cat kept stretching in the sun while we ate. I couldn't help looking at him. I filled a glass with water. The glass had some flowers painted in enamel color. They looked like daisies and dahlias. "Are dahlias poisonous?" "No," I thought, "but…"

Staring at the glass, I thought it would be easy to prepare a foxglove concoction and make her drink it. I drank the water, but I was still toying with the idea. I could cut up red rattles into pieces, and it would take only fifteen minutes to turn the liquid fatal. I would tell Nena about it, as we decorated her birthday cake. Then I would cook the liver the cat ate in this concoction.

I would bury the remains in the chestnut and bay trees outside my window. I could.

11

*I*rlanda and her white dresses. Always white. Always white. And the bright glow of her skin. She stayed at the door until very late that night, walking around, calling her cat. We saw her with a flashlight, a small silly fire, through the gallery, floating behind the windows like spirits misleading travelers, letting out dreadful screams, and moving away from their victims, drawing them toward the abyss. *I found a bad omen in my path, Mother. I don't know whether I'm alive or dead.*

"What have you done with my cat?" she asked, furious, shaking off the night dew. "What have you done with my cat?"

"What would she do?" said Roberto, putting out his cigarette. "Don't you see she's terrified of the cat? What's the matter with the women in this house? The cat must have gone outside to roam around. There are so many female cats out there. He'll show up tomorrow morning."

"My baby. My poor, poor baby," repeated Irlanda.

"Irlanda, that's enough for today. Leave a bowl of milk out for your baby and go to bed."

"I'll leave the door open."

"Don't even think about going near the door. If the cat doesn't show up tomorrow, we'll go look for him. We'll organize a search party. I'm even willing to call the police, but let me sleep tonight."

I left the kitchen in silence and went up the stairs with odd premonitions. The red room was next to Irlanda's, and it was almost as bright as hers. I sat on the edge of the bed, feeling dead tired. Irlanda came quietly into the room and walked toward me.

"I know you did something to my cat. I know it was you who spoiled my books and broke my parasol. I know all your tricks against me." She paused for a moment, then continued. "Who do you think you are? Have you ever looked at yourself in the mirror? Oh, you think you're smart, don't you? You think you're smarter than me? Huh? You don't have the slightest idea what life is all about," she said, with indifference. As she leaned over me, I saw her contracted pupils and the soft quiver of her eyebrows. "You with your stupid gifts, the stinking perfume you expected me to wear, and those cheap and badly cut clothes. And your ridiculous plants and your make-believe. I don't think you even know what I'm talking about. You live in your own little world, like a child shut away in a room full of toys. Nobody crosses me unless I let them."

I kept my mouth shut. Irlanda raised her head arrogantly.

"You're coming to my school this year. Don't try to deny it. I know it because my mother told me. If worst comes to worst, I'll ask you to come, and you'll do so. And your baby sister too. You know who I am at this school? I pity you. Who do you think ordered my girlfriends not to pay attention to you? They were glad they didn't have to deal with you."

She looked at me for a moment, and then continued.

"But they'll talk to you, you know. I won't say anything bad enough about you so they won't say hello to my two cousins. You'll be surrounded by boys who want to find out whether what's said about you is true. And they'll say, 'How odd! Irlanda is modest and reserved, but....' They'll want to know, and you'll know what it feels like to have to avoid them, and what it feels like to be a girl everyone talks about. I know how to do it. It wouldn't be the first time. Breaking my parasol!" she hissed. "You're acting like a baby. Why don't you grow up? You'll learn what revenge means when you come to my school," she said, making a charming gesture with her hand. "You have no idea what I'm capable of. And Gabriel...."

"Irlanda," said Roberto in the hallway. "Enough chatting. Go to bed."

"My cat had better show up tomorrow," she added, already at the door. "For your sake."

"You'll have to search through the bay trees," I thought. "He's used up all his nine lives this time." I heard Irlanda's door slam shut and closed my eyes. Her small pupils flashed before my mind, and I curled up under the blankets. If only the turtle didn't come back, if the blue cat and my sister's ghost didn't come back, I would be happy that night.

The chirping of crickets and the different bed kept me awake. My life was moving from one room to another. The cuckoo clock announced midnight, and I thought I heard Irlanda's door squeak softly. I sat up, expecting her to come back and threaten me again, but there were only the usual night sounds, and I went back to keeping away ghosts. The clock struck two, and then three. My eyelids were dropping, but the night after the cat's death was coming to a close, and his cunning spirit would lose most of its power to torment me after that night. During the day, there would be nothing to be afraid of.

Soon the morning would get light. I opened the window and let in the fresh morning air. At that moment, I saw, near the stable shed, the hoe I had used to dig among the bay trees. I opened my eyes wide. I had left it half hidden there, because when I left the woods, Roberto was coming back from his walk and would have been surprised to see me with a hoe in my hand. After dinner, I completely forgot about it after seeing Irlanda's flickering flashlight.

I threw my jacket over my shoulders to go down for the hoe. If I stayed asleep, Roberto would go out in the morning and find the hoe with the dirt redder than usual. I had to clean it and put it with the other hoes. I tiptoed across the creaking floor and slowly began turning the doorknob. Then Irlanda's door opened with a dull creak. I stepped back.

Gabriel slipped out of the room without a sound, smiling. Irlanda took his hand and stood on tiptoe to kiss him. Gabriel's shoulders and back had red marks, paths opened by Irlanda's fingernails. They moved apart. Gabriel caressed Irlanda's face and walked through the darkness toward his room. Irlanda closed the door, and I heard her muffled laughter.

And I had begged him to free me from my fate. Gabriel, who had pressed his flesh against Irlanda's during those nights, was already possessed by another kind of magic from which he wouldn't be free, Irlanda's gravity field. While I shut myself in my room to dream, she was tracing the path of Gabriel's spine with her fingers, digging her nails into his skin to leave marks, so that I would know in the morning that he had been hers.

It wasn't fair. His father's blood. Born into the other world. The dead snake at the road bend. His figure at the well, the red apples he picked for me. I couldn't breathe. I was choking. I ran to my room with fabric walls he ripped with his hands. I buried my head in my hands and swallowed my moans. My life had been shattered. The summer had faded away with a weak flicker of my hope and desire. That night had happened suddenly before the previous night, because it couldn't have happened, and now nothing would make time stop. Hours kept passing unchronologically, consequences had no importance, and actions meant nothing.

Suddenly, I no longer saw summer as the season of white roses, or the days when my heart burst until it turned pink and bled, but as a never-ending sequence of meaningless events. I had come and gone, opened and closed doors, gone outside and gone back inside the house. We had made our beds, and the sun had woken us, and we had done the same thing again after coming and going, opening and closing doors, going outside and going back into the house.

All of us had taken great pains to finish our chores, the boys cutting firewood and hammering nails, and Irlanda and I had been caught up in our war of flowers and dresses, like newly hatched butterflies under the ticking of the clock. The summer had been like that, and now autumn shortened the days, and the butterflies would be gone.

I stood in front of the mirror. The clear shadow escaped the mirror's foggy surface like chrysalises ready to hatch. I ran my hands down my hips and over my chest. My bones showed through my skin, and I traced the warm lines of my ribs. Now I was frail, as thin as Irlanda, with wrists as fragile as Gabriel's, as skinny as Sagrario had been when she plunged into death, but nothing had changed. My bones weren't as elegant as Irlanda's, my neck didn't straighten like hers, and I would never become like her. Instead, I would be a copycat with learned motifs, a cross between Sagrario and Irlanda, a creature living a life of borrowed actions and gestures, turning furiously from my north to my south, tired, as tired as I was feeling then.

There were no happy endings, there were no dances with mysterious princes with looks as calm as still water. Like Sagrario, I would never wake from my dream. Everything collapsed because the foundations were false, and it was useless to take refuge in nostalgia, because I could never turn back time, even though the clock face was round. The world, fear, stretched forth under the window like my new domain.

I needed something to ease the pain. I repeated my name many times, but then I remembered what it meant. I didn't want to suffer any new birth, and I shut up. But there was a time when my name summed up everything, and when saying my name would banish fear from my mind. It was a long time ago, a summer of menacing trees and nightmares, of dusks outside the window and dresses stolen from the chests of dead owners.

Now my name was the only thing I had left on the land that didn't belong to me, in a house that didn't belong to my family, outside the story of beautiful women, Hibernias and Irlandas, who had no qualms about branding their slaves. My name would be the only thing left after I was gone, floating like names, ideas, and real loves, which weren't nearly so easy as imagined ones from a bed in a balcony overlooking the park. Whether or not the turtle caught up with me, everything got complicated by the minute, and life that didn't allow me to take part in its rituals turned into a hostile terrain where the ghosts made way for Irlanda. She was right. I knew nothing about life. I only knew I had to win, but I was very tired of fighting. I wanted to go away. I wanted to finish once and for all.

I got dressed. I went down the stairs, not caring how much noise I made, and threw the hoe among the farming tools. I sat on one of the benches in the garden, shuddering from the cold, to watch daybreak for the first time that summer.

Curled up in one of the friar's chairs near the fireplace in the living room, I waited for Irlanda, who never got up early. I had caught a cold, and I wrapped myself in a blanket. Roberto persuaded me to sleep in the red room for the rest of my stay.

I looked down meekly when he reproached me for being pig-headed the day before.

"I'll never understand you girls," he finally said. "Even if I lived a hundred years, I'd never know what goes on inside your head."

Irlanda woke up around midday. She was humming in the shower, and I heard her coming down the stairs. I sat up in my chair.

"Irlanda," I called in a soft voice. "Come here, please."

She came near me and crossed her arms, staring straight at me. Finally, she sat in front of me to listen.

"Irlanda, stop. Stop doing this. I beg you on my knees. I broke your parasol, and left wine stains on your books. I also broke the hinges of the silver candy box, and I hid the white organza dress among old rags in the cellar." I didn't mention her cat. I didn't want to make things any worse. "I didn't touch it. I'll show you where it is. You can have my share of the chests if you like. The velvet cape you liked so much, it's yours. But don't say anything about us in school. Nena is only five and very shy. If she gets off to a bad start, she'll never be left alone. Please, Irlanda. Please."

My cousin raised her eyebrows. "What do you mean by 'stop doing this'? Have I ever hurt you? What have I done to you?"

"Irlanda, please."

"You'd better explain to me. Have I ever been mean to you? Haven't I let you stay with us during the whole summer? Haven't I been nice to you? You're the one who was out of line and plotted against me. You little hypocrite, what did you expect? Did you expect me to walk behind you like your maid? Is that it?"

"Forgive me," I begged again. "I have been used to doing as I please all my life. I don't know how to conduct myself with people. Please."

Irlanda raised her chin. "Asking forgiveness is easy. I want to see how you behave first. We'll see. We still have five days left.

If you think I forget things so easily, you're mistaken. There are mistakes you can't fix with words."

The strain and lack of sleep made my hands tremble. I got up to pick up another blanket and drink some hot milk. The sun came in through the gallery, and specks of dust swirled as they rose toward the light. Irlanda made a move to sit. Then she seemed to remember something and her eyes sparkled.

"Wait," she said. "Don't go. Look. Do you know who gave me this?"

With a triumphant look, she showed me Gabriel's medallion, a large green stone set in a simple style. I remembered the torn snake's eye staring at me through it the first time I talked to Gabriel in front of the old chestnut tree. That tree had gone dry.

"Gabriel," I said.

"Gabriel," she repeated. "He said he wanted to see his reflections on my white neck. He caressed the nape of my neck while he talked. You have no idea how soft his skin is. He has been spending nights in my room for weeks. You never suspected it, did you? He keeps me awake all night, whispering into my ear, fiddling with my hair. During the day he tells me he can smell my scent everywhere." She gave a false sigh. "I should have told you before. After all, we're cousins. I was about to tell you yesterday, but I think it's better this way. I was furious with you, and you might have thought I was just taking revenge on you. I know you wanted to be…" she paused, "his friend. And you almost had him." She came near me, without averting her eyes. "Now it's your turn to clench your fists."

I clenched my fists and bowed my head. I pictured the green stone buried for ages in earth-colored velvet, silently beating in time with Gabriel's heartbeat and waking on Irlanda's throat. If I touched it with my fingertip, it would dissolve into ashes, but no one waited on the other side. The time of the shadows adorned with ghost jewelries was over.

"But, anyway. Is it the candle's fault that it attracts moths?" she said, laughing.

She put the medallion back on. I remained quiet. My reaction disappointed her. But I nodded as she talked. I drew water from the well, even though it was her turn. I spent the rest of the morning following her, listening to her until Gabriel joined us, and I slipped away without being noticed. I gave her Grandmother's album.

Roberto was pleased to see us together, and rested his hands on our shoulders. "Now there's finally peace in the house. I was beginning to worry. Yesterday you were screaming like kids fighting over a toy. I don't know what's got into you."

Irlanda brushed his hand from her shoulder, feigning outrage. "You're such a busybody."

Roberto enjoyed the outing and kept talking during the meal. The boys had to fix the garden gate. He thought he had placed it the right way, but he had realized that the gate of the old orchard opened inward, and wanted to fix it.

"I hope we can sell this house once and for all. It gives nothing but work."

"Now everything is done."

"Has your cat turned up yet, Irlanda?"

"No, not yet."

Gabriel was distant again, lost as the long-gone summer days. He noticed that I was watching him, and he smiled at me weakly as the same way he moved sometimes. I felt Irlanda's gaze, so I looked away without returning his smile.

That afternoon, at siesta time, I went back to my plates and my herbarium. So many things moved me. The chestnut tree, the red earth, the glazed look in the cat's eyes, the well outside the window, and the taste of Gabriel trapped in the walls of the house. I spread the dried plants on the table and piled the sheets on the floor. I had fallen way behind. I smiled when I found the pressed foxglove flowers.

I got up and walked through the gallery. The nights were generous and bountiful, and that night seemed to start at six in the evening. Magpies flew over the roof, and I remembered the bird nest near the stable. I carefully closed the door and slipped out of the house through the rear door.

The magpies had died. I found them among the roots of the bay tree, two heaps of wet feathers. Only the cuckoo was in the nest, larger and fatter than before. I felt like throwing a stone at the nest. I had promised myself to look after the baby birds, but I had left them to die. Now their ghosts would join the creatures I killed—the crushed turtle, Sagrario after she had talked about how sweet it would be to die, smothering under the pillow I pressed against her face until she stopped moving, the cat realizing too late that the poison accelerated his heartbeat. All my ghosts.

I made my way to the chaotic garden. The blackberry bushes grazed my legs. I picked two milky-colored poppies and went to the wall under my window to see what had happened to the huge red cabbage. It had gone rotten. None of us liked the red cabbage. Further away I heard a screeching sound like a gate on loose hinges.

Irlanda had finished her siesta and was making coffee in the kitchen. She turned back when she heard me enter. She went back to the stove when she saw it was me. I approached her shyly and left the white poppies on the table. Then I arranged my plants on the plates.

My gesture seemed to soften Irlanda. She held the stems of the poppies over the fire and singed the edges so that they would stay fresh longer. She rested against the door of the living room with a cup of coffee in her hand.

"What are you doing?"

"The usual."

"The weeds."

I shut up. She stepped toward me, prancing around like a thoroughbred mare.

"I just got a letter. They're already preparing the autumn party. You know? I don't know whether I should take the dresses from the chest or go to the dressmaker for a new one. I think I'll keep Gabriel a while longer, and he's seen all the dresses. But nobody else has seen them, and I can imagine how my friends will react to the period dresses."

Irlanda had picked up a dried pansy and fiddled with it until she broke it. She raised her hand.

"I broke it," she said, still in the same voice. "Was it important?"

"I have more," I said. "Many more. It's a very common flower."

12

Irlanda shrugged. "Weeds all look the same to me."

I explained to her how I filled index cards and how I had to stick the pressed plants onto sheets. Irlanda's skirt stirred a breeze as she came and went, and I held my treasures down with my hands.

"They're very fragile," I said. "It wasn't a good idea to put them up in the tower. Sagrario and I started the collection a long time ago to enter a regional competition. We won again last year, and Sagrario collected the prize."

Make the skirt a little longer, Mama. I don't want to show my legs.

"But since I work less and less on it, it'll turn yellow in the sunlight or crumble in the wind," I sighed.

"You'd find a better place in the barn," she said. "It's dark and dry."

I had never thought of the barn before. The tower looked so

comfortable and lost in the air, close to heaven, that it was the best place for the harmless souls of the plants to leave the earth.

"Your father thought the same thing. I'll ask Roberto to help me with the flower presses."

"Roberto is busy. I'll help you if you like."

"You don't have to, Irlanda. It's not urgent. And they're as heavy as lead. Your father took them up to the tower."

"Yes, it's urgent. There's a reason I'm asking you," she said, arching a meaningful brow. "If I don't go with you, I won't have a good excuse to see him. You wouldn't want me strutting brazenly straight up to him, the way you did the other day when you went up the tower."

I understood. Gabriel and Roberto were mending the garden gate. From time to time the gate creaked in tune with their voices. I stole a glance at them as I passed, but they were busy with the iron gate, with their muscles contorted from its weight. They didn't like me, but they didn't kill me, even though they were strong enough to tear me apart. Then I understood how indifferent the world was. The boys didn't see us. Gabriel brushed his hair off his forehead, and I swallowed a sigh. Irlanda and I went up the tower and lifted the wooden flower presses. But we put them back on the floor. They were too heavy for us.

"What did I tell you?"

"It doesn't matter. Let's ask the boys to take them down to the barn. They can't say we didn't try."

She stared at her nail, which she had broken against the floor. The evening came, slipping along the mountains of the east. The wretched meadow would crack with Irlanda's frozen laughter, rising from the grass in the afternoon. Irlanda threw a quick glance toward the plants.

"I can't believe how much garbage you have gathered here."

"This is herb Robert," I said, pointing with one finger. "Those are pansies. Look, there are many. And many roses. And these leaves are from the chestnut tree on the road. As you see, they're already dry."

The air was delightful, fresh, even though I was haunted by memories of burning hell. A soft breeze caressed my face. I closed my eyes before the invisible dust in the wind forced tears out of them. Irlanda carefully picked up one of the pressed flowers. It was the white rose she had worn to the meadow. She didn't seem to recognize it, and left it where it was.

"I haven't been here since the night of the fireworks. After all, it's all in ruins. Grandmother had it closed off, like the chapel, because she thought it didn't match the rest of the estate. She was right. Fake gothic, filled with frills."

She leaned over the handrail, looking for the boys. I did, too.

"Look. I can't see them well," she said. "What are they doing now?"

The boys had lifted the gate into its hinges, and now began swinging it back and forth. I looked away. If they opened and shut the gate seven times, the cortege of the dark world would take the invitation in earnest and charge toward the iron gate. But it didn't matter, and the reality of this world was prevailing. I tried to push away my old thoughts. The boys stopped moving the gate after the fifth time.

"We shouldn't watch them from here," I said.

"Why not?"

"We shouldn't spy on them."

"I think they wouldn't mind. We're in the tower, taking the air, minding our own business. The boys, as far as I know, aren't doing anything embarrassing. Besides, they can't see us from where they are. Keep your voice down."

Irlanda ripped a piece of plaster off the wall and threw it away. It fell at Roberto's feet. He was startled, looked around, and returned to work. Irlanda laughed.

"My brother is completely stupid." She shook her head and

let the wind blow her hair. "It's perfect, isn't it?"

"What?" I asked, even though I was thinking of Gabriel.

"Everything. The world. The house at sunset. Birds flying. Life. Me."

"She shouldn't be so vain," I thought.

Irlanda fidgeted with the medallion, looking at it against the light. The stifling evening drew to a close, filled with ghostly reflections. She struggled to unclasp the medallion and untangled the chain from her hair. She placed the medallion on the handrail and rubbed her neck.

"It was too tight. It's so heavy. Gabriel says it's a genuine emerald."

I grabbed the medallion, rolling up the chain, and stared at it for a moment.

"It's beautiful," I said.

And with a hard blow into which I put all my strength, I pushed Irlanda toward the setting sun. The handrail gave way, and I fell across the remains of the balcony that went crumbling down. I heard an animal shriek and Gabriel's scream. The collapsed tower was still, as if waiting for the next move on the chessboard. For a moment, I thought Irlanda would remain there, frozen in mid-air right in front of me, as I would remember her later for a long time.

In my mind's ear, the chains tying her life to her body creaked. I heard them squeak and snap, the same sound as when my sister smothered under the pillow and then was silent. The pebbles were sliding under my hands, and for a moment, I thought I was falling, too, and that the path to the other side lay open before me, gently inviting me to go along. That was death, the soft mist along the path, amnesia, inertia. All pain would have ended if only I unclenched my hands and followed the path.

In the distance I heard Roberto leaping up three steps at a time. He pulled me up toward him, hurting my wrist. Then someone made the next move on the chessboard. Everything went back to normal, the clocks began ticking at their normal pace, and the colors, smells, and noises assaulted me. I realized then, as if struck by a savage blow, that I was alive. I looked down. The path had disappeared. The grass still remained in its place, and shards of broken glass from the chapel window lay scattered across it. I pretended to sob, and nothing spoiled my satisfaction at seeing Irlanda's beautiful body broken.

That's how the summer ended. My aunt and uncle had the chapel and tower razed to the ground and quickly got rid of the farm. We rarely saw them again. They tried to forget that they had once had a family, and that one family member was missing. We suggested they should spend some time resting in the country, but they didn't heed our advice. Of course, this time they were the ones who had lost a daughter.

My parents were in tears when they saw me alive. They looked worried, as I eagerly described how blood had oozed from Irlanda's shuttered body. My mother repeated again and again that we had already suffered enough, and that we deserved a rest. Nena took me by the hand, whispered in my ear, and waited for the moment when we were alone, so I could tell her the whole story.

Roberto studied some kind of engineering and married the mawkish blonde right after his graduation. He never put on weight, grew a mustache like his father, and took charge of the construction of the new neighborhood in the village, which finally began and only served to perpetuate the dreadful legends about our family among the whole village, old and young. None of us cared very much, though, as the villagers had always hated us.

Gabriel survived only for a short time. In the end, he was driven to destruction by the same impulses that ruined his father. He turned into a pale ghost with slashed wrists and courted schoolgirls only to let them starve to death. He disappeared silently, like everything that comes from another world. I learned of his death when I hadn't had any news of him in a long time. I had thought he was safe from danger, forever mingling with common men who adored lively pretty women and didn't waste their time searching through the glass cabinets of death.

We never talked again. When we sat down together, neither of us had anything to say. I saw him once, lost in the shadows of the school hallway, wandering aimlessly, casting no shadow, the grass rustling in an invisible breeze. I waved him over, but he turned his back and walked away with the same drowsy air he had when he was alive. When my heart was filled with bitterness and my hands longed for his distant smile and the immortal gesture of his neck, I would bring the medallion to my mouth and bite it, as its green stone shone, like an old friend who gave me a wink.

Nena and I were warmly received, as heirs to the affection Irlanda had inspired in everyone who knew her. There were birthday parties and a dance every spring and every fall, unexpected declarations of love, and inexorable refusals.

The mawkish blonde who would become my cousin tried to form a clique around me, but she gave up because of my retiring nature and stubborn devotion to my family and my plants. In spite of everything, some things stayed the same. Curiosity soon died away, and we could enjoy again our former peaceful life. Gradually, we fell into a routine, and time became meek, circling around my path with no surprises and no frights.

We built Irlanda a grave with a cross and a white marble stone. She was buried after a service at the packed church, and many flowers on her grave, and then nothing. Her girlfriends and admirers, including the boy with the white rose who wept at the burial and later courted me for years, belonged to life, the same life of grownups who kept going in the world without worrying about anything other than what she had longed for.

To comfort her in her solitude, I visited her more often than I visited my sister Sagrario, who was happy dancing in the green fields around the country house, lost among the bay trees and ash trees. Sagrario had taken with her the turtle, the cat, and the baby magpies, looking after them with devotion. They followed her everywhere she went, watching her from a distance when she danced. But Irlanda didn't dance anymore.

During whole afternoons, I sat by the angel on her grave. Nena played, making wreaths of flowers. She would ask me about the tower, about Irlanda's cat, about the torn heart of the red cabbage, about how I had ended Sagrario's suffering, and about the ghosts of that summer, even though my parents never approved of my stories. They wanted her to watch more TV, and always asked me to read to her stories about girls devoured by wolves and stepmothers who fed poisoned apples to beautiful stepdaughters. Sometimes I told her the stories my parents preferred, but only when we were in the cemetery, sitting on Irlanda's tombstone. Irlanda had never liked fairy tales.

As Nena ran among the graves with an arum lily in her hands, frightening away cats, I talked to the angel who watched over my cousin to keep her from coming back to life, fluttering his feathered wings to make time pass faster. He didn't have to work very hard, because Irlanda would never appear anywhere looking the way death had disfigured her. But wanting to please her, I updated her on how Armando's courtship was coming along, told her how I was pampered in school, and let her know how grateful I was for her legacy. My own sister had left me only her love for a boy who read in the park, but as in everything else, Irlanda had easily surpassed her. I was careful not to soil her immaculate new house with red dirt, as she would hate to see anything white get dirty.

There we buried her memory and her cold eyes. There she lived forever, never coming back, never visiting me in my dreams, trapped in the labyrinth of paths I had been weaving for her for a long time, with so much care and affection, with the new spirits of my nights.

the end

TRANSLATOR'S NOTE

Espido Freire was born in Bilbao, Spain, in 1974, of Galician parents. She received a bachelor's degree in English philology and a master's degree in editing from the University of Deusto, where she also founded and edited literary journals. In 1998, she made her literary debut with the novel *Irlanda*. In 1999, the French version of the novel won France's Prix Millepages for Best Foreign Fiction. Freire is the author of several novels, including *Donde siempre es octubre* (1999), *Melocotones helados* (winner of the 1999 Premio Planeta), and *Nos espera la noche* (2003), as well as story collections *Juegos míos* (2004) and *El trabajo os hará libres* (2008). In 2007, she won the Premio Ateneo de Sevilla for her novel *Soria Moria*. Her novels have been translated into over a dozen languages, including French, German, and Portuguese. Excerpts from *Irlanda* have been published in my translations: the first chapter appeared in the Violet Issue of *Fairy Tale Review*, the second chapter in the Summer 2007 issue of *The Modern*

Review, and the third chapter in the December 2008 issue of *Words Without Borders*. My translations of her short stories have appeared in *The Dirty Goat*, *Gargoyle Magazine*, and *Metamorphoses*.

I was drawn to *Irlanda* partly because I have had a favorable impression of Spain ever since I first visited the country in 2000. Although I could not have internalized the cadence of the language only after a few weeks' stay, my trips to Spain paid off in some way, as I felt a deep psychological connection to the novel while translating it. Although I have not returned to Spain since June 2001, I still feel a strong affinity with the country and its people. This may be one of my little quirks, but I very rarely translate a text from a country I have never been to. All the writers I regularly translate are from countries I have visited at least twice—Mexico, Spain, and Peru.

The gender of the author also influenced my decision to translate *Irlanda*, as I consciously choose to translate women writers. In Spain, the emergence of women writers has largely coincided with the post-Franco democratization, which has enabled women to play a more active role in society. For this reason, the presence of women is felt strongly among Spanish writers born in the 1960s and '70s.

Unlike most writers of her generation, who tend to favor gritty urban realism, Freire infuses her fictional worlds with magical qualities, as she does in *Irlanda*. In fact, Freire's novels are more akin to those of the "Boom" writers of Latin America, who popularized magical realism in the 1960s, than to those of her Spanish contemporaries. *Irlanda* tells the story of Natalia, a fifteen-year-old girl with a strong imagination. Transplanted to the run-down family estate, she has to deal with her sister Sagrario's ghost, her infatuation with a boy named Gabriel, and her "perfect" cousin Irlanda.

Like her other novels, *Irlanda* shows Freire's preoccupation with fairy tales. In this modern, dark retelling of fairy tales, the good does not always triumph over the evil, as the line between the two forces is blurred in her fictional world. Natalia reacts to her surroundings and events in her life through the lens of the fairy tale. As she encounters spirits in trees, meadows, and streams, the ghosts of dead animals torment her in dreams.

Since *Irlanda*, Freire has repeatedly used fairy tales as motifs in her fiction. For instance, her 2003 novel, *Nos espera la noche*, takes place in Gyomaendrod, a mystical land where five families struggle for power. Even in her nonfictional writings, Freire takes fairy tales as her point of departure, as she did in her 2000 nonfiction book, *Primer amor*, which explores first love.

The first seeds of her novels probably took root during her childhood, as Freire grew up listening to her Galician grandmother's stories. Perhaps because of this, her novels have a timeless feel to them, even when they are set in modern times. *Irlanda* is no exception, as it hardly contains a reference that dates the novel.

Freire has a knack for creating a darkly nuanced atmosphere in her narrative. The difficulty of translating *Irlanda*, which is otherwise easy to translate, arises from the fact that the novel constantly blurs the line between reality and fantasy. The translator needs to preserve the magical qualities of the novel without explaining away too much.

A prolific writer who works in multiple genres, Freire is considered one of the most important writers in Spain today. As a novice translator, I was apprehensive about approaching such an accomplished author. Fortunately, Freire has turned out to be an ideal original author. Her compliments on my translations mean the world to me because she is a literary translator herself and fluent in English. Thanks to the aforementioned publications, I had the honor of introducing Freire to English-speaking readers. I look forward to translating her other novels.

THREE APPRECIATIONS OF *IRLANDA*

The Deceptive Simplicity of Espido Freire's *Irlanda*
By Tom Whalen

The elements of Espido Freire's first novel *Irlanda*, translated
from the Spanish by Toshiya Kamei, are, like all great fairy tales,
deceptively simple. After the long illness and death of Sagrario,
one of her two younger sisters, Natalia is sent by her mother to
spend the summer helping her two teenage cousins, Roberto
and the beautiful, "perfect" Irlanda, and Gabriel, a friend of Roberto's, do minor repairs to the family's decaying country house
whose "tower and chapel, with their medieval facades, stood
crumbling, crawling with vermin." Family rivalry, displacement,
jealousy, loss of an inheritance and of a sister—like musical
themes the elements fall quickly into place and are kept in play
by Freire's uncanny ability to inhabit the mind and universe of
an adolescent, to capture the texture of her days.

> It was my first time to go to the country all by myself, but
> I didn't think of that until much later. As I pressed my
> forehead against the cold window, it struck me that I had

already lived through this. During most of my trip, I knew all my movements in advance, as if a strange vision was telling me what would come next. It was just like those dreams that turned into nightmares, and I was afraid everything was the turtle's trick to seize me while I slept. I said my name seven times, and the strange feeling began to lift. I opened my eyes again and found myself on the way to the country house.

Natalia is highly imaginative and, as we're made quickly aware, somewhat disturbed. "When I was little, I imagined that the branches sticking into the sky were goblins' arms trying to snatch me away. I closed my eyes and thought about Sagrario. Somewhere on this earth, she raised her feeble arms, petrified in an oak tree." Like her dead sister, the turtle in the passage above is another ghost or demon dreamed into being by Natalia after its death. When she kills Sagrario's pet, Natalia "buried my favorite doll and the most beautiful marble in my collection in a box, hoping to appease the turtle," which still doesn't stop it from becoming the *bête noir* in her (sleeping or waking) dreams.

The seeming simplicity of Freire's prose quivers, wobbles— and suddenly we're dropped into psychological depths found only in the best novels about children. Somewhere between the languid mysteries of Alain-Fournier's *Le Grand Meaulnes* and the hard-earned surrealism of Margarita Karapanou's *Kassandra and the Wolf* resides *Irlanda*'s special contribution to this subgenre. More slyly, as the narrative develops, *Irlanda* touches hands with the masterworks of another subgenre, tales narrated by the mad, from Poe to Nabokov. And, gliding along the surface of the gorgeously clear (and gorgeously translated) prose, slipping into the consciousness of an adolescent girl, you don't notice that the plot is as finely honed as, say, one by Highsmith or Boileau & Narcejac.

Sentences like "The leaves danced in the wind, and showed their pale bellies, as if embarrassed, outside the windows" and

"The pages curled up at the edges, as if complaining about the treatment they received" pleasantly surprise us with their personifications, while masking, for a moment, how strange the child who thought them is. Natalia's narration is not only a miracle of style, but of perfectly timed releases of plot points. Sagrario, her death, her turtle, Natalia's herbarium, chess, old dresses, Irlanda's blue cat—all the novel's motifs intensify as they accumulate and reveal more and more their importance to Natalia's story.

Irlanda also exhibits a rarely seen reflexive elegance. Our two princesses will have their final battle in the tower that's "in ruins" as Irlanda says, adding, "Fake gothic, filled with frills." Exasperated with Natalia's fantasies, Irlanda tells her, "I've never known anyone so obsessed with fairy tales. You can be so childish sometimes." "I'll never understand you girls," Roberto tells Natalia and his sister. "Even if I lived a hundred years, I'd never know what goes on inside your head."

The minds of the mad, as Poe's gothic narratives show, don't necessarily degenerate into chaos; they can obtain a heightened sense of clarity where everything shimmers with meaning. No matter that Roberto tells Natalia, "You're crazy! Completely nuts!" or Irlanda, possessed by her own adolescent vindictive madness, says "You live in your own little world, like a child shut away in a room full of toys," Natalia knows better. To give up her fantasy world would be to admit that her days were "a never-ending sequence of meaningless events." By transforming her reality she keeps the dead alive and her guilt at bay. Even the mad, after all, can be realists and understand "how indifferent the world was."

> There were no happy endings, there were no dances with mysterious princes with looks as calm as still water. Like Sagrario, I would never wake from my dream. Everything collapsed because the foundations were false, and it was

useless to take refuge in nostalgia, because I could never turn back time, even though the clock face was round. The world, fear, stretched forth under the window like my new domain.

Irlanda is a brilliantly perverse fairy tale and Espido Freire a master prestidigitator who hides until the end exactly how perverse her novel really is. There *is* a "happy" ending, of course, with *happy* written in the kind of dark comic irony one finds in the novels of Russell H. Greenan. When you finish reading *Irlanda*, go back to the beginning: "Sagrario died in May, after much suffering." I've never read a more troubling comma than the one that cracks open this simple sentence.

In Praise of *Irlanda*
By Suzanne Kamata

Before Toshiya Kamei's translation of *Irlanda*, I'd never heard of Espido Freire. Sadly, we Americans are always the last to know what's happening literarily in other countries. Freire, I later found out, has achieved celebrity status in her native Spain, and was awarded the Millepage Prize by the French for *Irlanda*, her debut novel, published when she was just twenty-four.

The narrator, Natalia, is fifteen years old, "a mischievous girl with a strong imagination." The novel opens shortly after the burial of Sagrario, her beloved younger sister, who has died after a prolonged illness. Natalia has a special bond with her remaining sister, five-year-old Nena, but she doesn't have any companions her own age. "I'd never had girlfriends," she says. "I didn't need them. Once I had played on the beach with a girl who let me borrow her bucket and shovel, and we jumped the waves together. But I never saw her again." Apparently, the company of her sisters had been enough, but with the loss of Sagrario, they are enveloped in grief. They spend their time pressing funeral flowers and reading Sagrario's diaries.

Natalia is haunted by ghosts of animals, and also her dead sister. The appearance of a phantom turtle evokes Latin American magical realism, or perhaps Edgar Allan Poe. And then there is Nena's disturbing preoccupation with poisonous plants. The reader gets a sense that this family is by no means ordinary. Warped by grief and suffering, they have been isolated, at a remove from the rest of society. Natalia's parents decide that a summer in the country with cousin Irlanda would be therapeutic for her. So she is sent to the crumbling estate to help clean it, and perhaps prepare it for sale.

Irlanda is beautiful and popular—but sometimes cruel. When her prep school friends are around, she more or less ignores Natalia. However, after Irlanda's classmates leave, the cousins talk about boys and try on dresses, but their girl-talk is far from typical. When speaking of Gabriel, a boy Natalia believes to be close to the spirit world, she refers to his "demented eyes."

The story is set in the present—there are references to television and a drug bust and teen magazines—but the setting—an old house filled with cobwebs and a trunk full of antique gowns—as well as Natalia's quaint pressing of flowers and handing out bouquets, and the elegant simple prose itself, seem to put the story at a remove from modern times. Events could be unfolding in another realm—that of the fairy tales Natalia references, for example. Although the setting is in some ways bucolic, a sense of foreboding infuses these pages. The reader just knows something bad is going to happen by the end of summer. When it does, it comes as the inevitable, yet surprising ending that all good novels ought to have.

Like Amelie Nothumb, another young European writer who has found fans through translation in the States, Freire's voice is fresh and subversive. I predict her appeal will transcend borders.

Kamei has already proven himself as a champion of young Hispanic women writers and as a skilled wordsmith with his translation of Liliana Blum's *The Curse of Eve and Other Stories* (Host Publications, 2008). Readers of English are now lucky to have a chance to read Kamei's deft rendering of *Irlanda*.

A Magical Tale
By Molly Giles

Two years ago I had the pleasure of serving on Toshiya Kamei's thesis committee. Toshiya Kamei had been in several of my graduate fiction writing classes and had, in fact, translated several of my own stories into Spanish for publication in magazines like *Opcion* and *Literal*. To defend his MFA degree in translation, he submitted his translation of an amazing novel, *Irlanda*, by a young Spanish writer I had never before heard of, Espido Freire.

This was my loss, for Freire, barely thirty years old, is well known outside the United States for her four novels, two collections of stories, and a memoir. *Irlanda*, her first novel, was written when she was only twenty-four. It's a magical tale told in the classic style—a young girl is exiled to a forbidding place where she is haunted by ghosts, taunted by rivals, and troubled by love. The writing is spare, clean, and lyrical, the pacing is swift, the mood is... Spanish! How to explain. There is a somber, slumberous, strong human life to the story. Because my knowledge of contemporary Spanish literature is so thin, I think of films. Movies like *The Orphanage* or *Pan's Labyrinth* capture the same sense of the ethereal and the earthy that I found in *Irlanda*, and the free, imaginative, often comical leaps of Almodovar films also come to mind. I suspect *Irlanda* will in time make a great little movie, but in the meantime, as a book, it is compelling enough.

It is a book that my American students would adore. Graduate students are huge fans of writers like Neil Gaiman and Kelly Link, both of whom are labeled "dark," both of whom are labeled "fantasy writers," and both of whom are akin to Espido Freire in the style, sense, and spirit. I know that Toshiya Kamei's wonderful translation of this book will appeal to a wide audience.

BIOS

Espido Freire made her literary debut with the novel *Irlanda* in 1998. It has been translated into several languages; this is the exclusive English-language edition. The French version of the novel, translated by Eva Calveyra, won the Millepage Prize in France. In 1999, she was awarded the Premio Planeta for her novel *Melocotones helados*. She is the youngest writer to have won this well-funded literary award. Her novels have been translated into several languages, including French, German, Turkish, Dutch, Italian, Polish, Portuguese, Chinese, and Japanese. In 2007, she won the Premio Ateneo de Sevilla for her novel *Soria Moria*.

Toshiya Kamei is the translator of *The Curse of Eve and Other Stories* (2008) by Liliana Blum and *La Canasta: An Anthology of Latin American Women Poets* (2008), as well as selected works by Édgar Omar Avilés. He is also translator of Naoko Awa's *The Fox's Window and Other Stories* (University of New Orleans Press, 2009).

Tom Whalen's books include *Elongated Figures* (Red Dust), *Winter Coat* (Red Dust), *Roithamer's Universe* (Portals Press), *Dolls* (Caketrain Press), and *An Exchange of Letters* (Parsifal Press). His collaborative translations of stories by Robert Walser are in *Selected Stories* (Farrar, Straus, Giroux; Vintage; New York Review Books) and *Masquerade and Other Stories* (Johns Hopkins University Press), and he co-edited the Robert Walser issue of *The Review of Contemporary Fiction*. *The Birth of Death and Other Comedies: The Novels of Russell H. Greenan* is forthcoming from Dalkey Archive in 2011. He teaches American literature at the University of Stuttgart and film at Staatliche Akademie der Künste Stuttgart. (www.tomwhalen.com)

Suzanne Kamata is the author of *Losing Kei*. She was born and raised in Grand Haven, Michigan. She is most recently from Lexington, South Carolina, and now lives in Tokushima Prefecture, Japan, with her husband and two children. She edits and publishes the literary magazine *Yomimono*.

Molly Giles was nominated for a Pulitzer Prize for fiction for her first book, *Rough Translations*, which also won the Pushcart Prize, the Flannery O'Connor Award for Short Fiction, the Small Press Book Award, the Boston Globe Award, the Bay Area Book Reviewers Award, and the PEN Syndicated Fiction Award. Her second book, another collection of short stories, is called *Creek Walk*, and was named one of the *New York Times'* most notable books of 1997. Giles is currently Professor and Director of Programs in Creative Writing at the University of Arkansas.

ACKNOWLEDGMENTS
Toshiya Kamei, Translator

Excerpts from this novel have appeared in the following magazines: *Fairy Tale Review*, *The Modern Review*, and *Words Without Borders*.

I would like to thank the following people who have contributed to this project at different stages of its development: Hilda Benton, Kate Bernheimer, Molly Giles, Susan Harris, Suzanne Kamata, and Tom Whalen.

FAIRY TALE REVIEW · PRESS

*"There are fairy tales to be written for adults,
fairy tales almost blue."*

— ANDRE BRETON

Fairy Tale Review Press is dedicated to helping raise public aware-
ness of the literary and cultural influence of fairy tales, and to
appreciating their power and depth as an art form. It celebrates
fairy tales as one of our oldest and most underestimated plea-
sures. Fairy Tale Review Press seeks to improve the critical un-
derstanding of new works sewn from fairy tales and welcomes
the public to revisit old tales across borders and time, to celebrate
their transfixing power and protect them for future generations of
readers. Fairy Tale Review Press also publishes *Fairy Tale Review*,
an annual journal. Fairy Tale Review Press invites your letters and
comments.

Please write to: FAIRYTALEREVIEW@GMAIL.COM

OTHER PUBLICATIONS BY
FAIRY TALE REVIEW · PRESS

Fairy Tale Review
The Blue Issue (2005)
The Green Issue (2006)
The Violet Issue (2007)
The White Issue (2008)
The Aquamarine Issue (2009)
The Red Issue (2010)

PILOT ("Johann the Carousel Horse")
POETRY
by Johannes Göransson
ISBN: 978-0-9799954-1-5

THE CHANGELING
FICTION
by Joy Williams
ISBN: 978-0-9799954-0-8

CHANGING: A NOVELLA
FICTION
by Lily Hoang
ISBN: 978-0-9799954-2-2

WHITEWORK
POETRY
by Ashley McWaters
ISBN: 978-0-9799954-3-9